BECAUSE SHE COULD

By

Kaylie Kay

ISBN:
ISBN-13: **9781982916909**

DEDICATION

For Olivia xxx.

CONTENTS

ACKNOWLEDGMENTS

To my friends who have allowed me to put you in my book, albeit exaggerated forms of yourselves, I thank you. Julie, I can only apologise, but it has caused me much amusement to write your scenes!

I thank too the crew who have listened to me talk about the book, in the middle of the night at 39,000 feet, for your enthusiasm and encouragement gave me the energy to keep writing. For those of you who read it in your hotel rooms downroute and told me you loved it when we checked out, you have no idea how much your kind words meant to me.

Olivia, one day you will be old enough to read it. Thank you for letting me use your name – I hope you like your namesake!

All of the characters are fictitious, unless I have told you that you are in it, and so too are the airline, hotels and events.

Chapter 1

'Well good evening, ladies and gentlemen, and a very warm welcome onboard this Osprey Aviation flight OS908 to Hong Kong.' Olivia knew the boarding announcement off by heart, and she also knew that nobody was listening to her right now. As she told them about restrictions on using their electronics, and whether or not their seatbelts contained an airbag, they were far too busy finding room in the overhead lockers to stow their luggage, and making claim to what was going to be their personal space for the next eleven and a half hours, to listen to what she was saying.

It was almost 10pm, half an hour until the scheduled departure time, and Olivia was pleased to see that most of them looked weary, just like her. From her door at the rear left of the aircraft she watched them flow into the cabin, and slowly take their seats. They seemed to be mostly young and Chinese, probably university students going home for the summer, it was July after all, she mused, continuing with her announcement mindlessly.

'Captain Barnes informs us that the flight time tonight will be a little over eleven and a half hours and reminds you that smoking is not allowed on board…' Blah, blah, blah. Still they continued to board, and still no one was listening as Olivia finished the PA and hung up her handset.

Twenty-eight years old and Olivia Kaye had been crew for Osprey almost all of her working life, it was all that she knew, and she had worked her way up to purser at the airline. She loved her job and the lifestyle that it gave her, even now when she could feel the tiredness creeping up and the long night stretched ahead.

The butterflies in her stomach reminded her that she was going to the city she loved most in the world, but even they felt a little fatigued right now. She wondered what this trip would hold when they got there, what she would get up to on the two-night layover. Would it be as good as her last trip here? What would the crew that she had only met an hour or so before be like once they were out of their smart navy uniforms? One thing she did know already was that the flight would be easy enough, these always were, and for that she was grateful. She'd take this over a party flight to Las Vegas any day!

She looked longingly at the locked door to her right, in the middle of the galley. Behind it lay the staircase which led up to every flight attendant's favourite place, the crew rest area. Oh, how she wanted to be in that bunk up there right now, under that duvet, sinking her head into that big feather pillow! *Just three hours,* she thought to herself, then the meal service would be over and breaks could start.

As the cabin filled up Olivia's attention was caught by a western family struggling down the left-hand aisle. The dad led the way, towering over the smaller Chinese passengers around him. He carried a bag over each of his broad shoulders, no doubt full of everything they would need to survive the flight, and a small boy, perhaps two years old, clung to his neck. Without a spare hand to push it away, his mop of thick, dark, wavy hair fell forward into his eyes. He stopped and placed the child into his seat, before scraping it back with open fingers, clearly relieved to be able to see properly again. She watched him drop the bags onto the floor and stretch briefly before bending back down.

Behind him Olivia could now see a petite lady who looked slightly older than him, dressed sensibly in black trousers and floral blouse, with a neat blonde bob. She seemed flustered as she ushered a second child, a young fair-haired girl of three or four, ahead of her whilst pulling a small case behind. Olivia's heart went out to them, it was hard enough flying long-haul with small children, let alone so late at night with such young ones.

'Can you watch my door, hon?' she called to the girl who was busy preparing carts in the galley. She wanted to go and offer them some help but it was strictly forbidden to leave a door unattended on the ground. Rules were rules.

'Of course,' said the other girl. Olivia thought her name was Alex, but wasn't quite sure enough to call her by name yet, so 'hon' or 'babe' would suffice until she could get a proper look at her name badge. With thousands of crew it was impossible to know everyone, and whilst she had flown with a couple of them on today's flight before, the rest were just new allies to be made.

'Excuse me, sir, excuse me,' she chanted as she made her way up past the people standing in the aisles, grateful that she was slim and able to squeeze past them. When she eventually made it to row 43, where the family had stopped, she watched in amusement for a brief moment as the lady busily unpacked her bag in her seat. She hadn't noticed that as quick as she was stuffing essentials into their seat pockets, the youngest child was pulling it all back out again. The man, meanwhile, was playing the overhead locker game, arranging and rearranging the bags to make them fit, muttering under his breath, clearly annoyed.

'Can I help you at all?' Olivia asked.

'No, we're fine,' came the curt reply, without so much as a look in her direction. 'Dammit,' he cursed, shoving one of the bags angrily when it still wouldn't fit.

The lady looked up at Olivia and gave her a weak smile. She was definitely older than the man now that she could see her up close, the lines around her eyes forged by the extra years. Olivia was struck by how beautiful she still was though, with high cheekbones and perfect teeth, and she hoped that she would be fortunate enough to age so well.

'Thank you for the offer, I think we are ok though,' she said kindly.

'Ok, well let me know if there is anything we can do for you,' Olivia replied earnestly before turning back around. 'There is space in the locker opposite, sir,' she said over her shoulder as she walked away. If he had just taken a deep breath, instead of getting all stressed out, he might have noticed that the locker on the other side was half empty. Had he been an ounce of polite Olivia may have stayed and helped him stow his bags, but she was damned if she was going to now.

'Are they ok?' asked Alex when she got back to the door.

Olivia took a sly look at her badge and confirmed her name.

'Mmm, I think they're just a bit stressed with the little ones. He's a bit rude though.'

'You can't help some people,' Alex sighed. 'Never mind, it's his problem, don't let it get to you.' She had obviously seen the frown on Olivia's face.

Normally Olivia didn't let rude passengers get to her. She had learnt not to take things personally. *You are just a uniform,* she would remind herself. Maybe it was because it was so late that she was being more sensitive tonight, but the man had really annoyed her; she had only wanted to help.

'Cabin crew, arm your doors.'

The announcement snapped her out of her blackening mood and back to reality; she had a job to do and a long night ahead.

As they taxied to the runway Olivia quickly took her phone out of her handbag, glancing first at her reflection in the blank screen and fastening the piece of her long dark hair that had escaped back with a grip.

Bye babe, love you xxxx, she texted.

She always sent a message to Tom before she left, always the same four words, and he always sent the same message back.

Love you too, miss you already xxxxx. It came straight back. She smiled and switched her phone off, dropped it into her handbag and stuffed the bag into the small cupboard opposite her jumpseat.

As she strapped into her seat she could hear a child crying. She hadn't seen any others boarding so she was almost certain it was one of the poor mites with the grumpy father. A small part of her felt sorry for them, but she couldn't help thinking that he deserved the extra stress for being so rude to her! As usually happened, by the time they took off and the landing gear was up the vibrations of the aircraft had calmed them and the crying had stopped. Hopefully they would sleep through the night now, for their sake and for the other passengers!

Chapter 2

'What can I get you for dinner, sir?'

'Would you like wine with your meal?'

The family had all been asleep as she passed them with the meal service, they were obviously exhausted. She felt her annoyance subside as she watched the youngest child sucking gently on his dummy, with his father's arm wrapped protectively around him. The daughter slept soundly with her head on the lap of the lady, her grandmother perhaps, she thought. She smiled at the tranquil scene and moved on to the next row.

The dinner service was over quickly. So many of the passengers were already sleeping, and as she turned the lights off in the cabin only the glare of a few TV screens broke the darkness.

Just as they were putting the last few things away the flight manager, Julie, floated into the galley in a waft of expensive perfume. Everyone at Osprey knew Julie Margot, even if they had never flown with her before. She was an icon at the airline, there since the start-up twenty-five years before. She was probably in her mid-fifties, but it was hard to tell thanks to the cosmetic procedures so popular with people in this industry, and with a size eight figure any twenty-year-old would die for, she was clearly not ready to give in to ageing any time soon.

Rumour was that she had once had an affair with the founder of the airline, back in its small and glamorous days, before it became the corporate machine that it was now. Apparently he had bestowed gifts of cars and jewellery on her to keep her silence and not kiss and tell, and she had been promoted through the ranks *very* quickly. In the years since the affair had run its course there had been allegations against her for all sorts of misconduct: turning up for work inebriated, inappropriate behaviour downroute, the list went on. Yet here she still was, apparently untouchable, and Olivia couldn't help but like her.

'Wow! That was quick, everyone. Well done!'

'Easiest service ever,' gushed Flic, the tall blonde girl working in the other aisle.

'Well I think we all deserve a break then.'

Julie began writing times and names down in her small red notebook.

Result, thought Olivia, watching over her shoulder. First break, three hours. She was so ready for it; it was nearly 1am and she could sleep standing up right now.

'Thanks, Jules. Goodnight all,' she called cheerily and opened the door that led up to the crew rest area, followed eagerly by the rest of the crew going on break now. She climbed the steps quickly and crawled into the middle bunk at the front, her favourite of the six that sat three either side of the stairwell. In her early flying days Olivia had found the crew bunks claustrophobic, with their low ceilings and narrow walls, but it was funny how you just got used to things. She removed her shoes and skirt, switched out her light and fell fast asleep in a matter of minutes.

Three hours seemed to pass in a flash.

'Time to get up,' came a soft voice over the PA.

Ugh.

Olivia rubbed her eyes and took a moment to come round.

Back down in the galley, she hugged her mug of tea as she tried to wake up. She hated those happy morning people that could just bounce out of bed; she was definitely not one of those. The other crew had disappeared into the restrooms to sort themselves out, leaving her on her own to cheer up.

'Excuse me,' came a voice from behind her.

Seriously, she thought. *Go… away!*

She turned slowly and was surprised to see the father from the beginning of the flight standing behind her. Olivia would never have made it as a poker player, and she was quite sure that the look on her face was telling him that he was an unwelcome guest.

'So sorry to bother you but any chance of a coffee?' He ran his fingers through his hair and grinned sheepishly at her.

'Milk and sugar?' she asked abruptly.

'Just milk, please.'

Well at least he was remembering his manners now, she thought, somewhat appeased. Her displeasure was subsiding quickly; he was far too handsome to be annoyed with, all chiselled jaw and dark eyes, with long black eyelashes that she would die for.

She made his coffee and handed it to him.

'Thanks so much, I really appreciate it. Sorry about earlier, I was really stressed when I got on.'

'No problem.' He obviously knew that he had upset her, and she accepted his apology. 'Are the children still sleeping?'

'Yes, thank God,' he replied.

'Tough, huh, flying with little ones?'

He nodded, rolling his huge dark brown eyes upwards.

Olivia was becoming intrigued by this man and wanted to know more, starting with who the lady was that was with him.

'At least you have someone to help you.'

'My mother,' he offered. 'She's a saint, I don't know what I'd do without her.'

Interesting, so what about the children's mother? Olivia was naturally nosey, although she preferred to call it *interested*. Maybe that was too forward a question to ask though.

'Are you going on holiday?' she asked.

'No, I work out there, I'm a doctor,' he said matter-of-factly.

'Oh, wow.' Olivia was impressed, even if he wasn't. He was both handsome and successful.

'Yeah, I've been out here three years now, we've just been home for a couple of weeks.'

'So is your mum coming out on holiday?' *We will get there in a minute*, she thought, getting impatient now.

'No, she lives with me.' He paused, as if he wasn't sure if he should go on or not, looking down at his coffee for a moment before starting again. 'My wife passed away last year and Mum has moved out for a while to help look after the children.'

Well she hadn't expected that. Olivia suddenly wished she hadn't been so 'interested' because now she felt really bad. He was looking at her as if trying to read her reaction.

'Oh, I'm so sorry.' It was all she could think of to say, and she struggled to make eye contact for the first time since he had come in.

'Hey, it's fine. Thanks for the coffee, I'd better get back in case one of them wakes up,' he said gratefully as he turned around and walked back towards his seat with his drink.

Poor, poor man, she thought. *Poor handsome, gorgeous man!*

Chapter 3

Jeremy Holland, or Jez to everyone who knew him, sat in the front seat of the cab and watched his two children gently dozing in the back, under the watchful eye of his mother. He honestly didn't know how he'd have coped without her since Vanessa's death, unsure if he would actually have coped at all.

Three years ago when they had first arrived in Hong Kong, they had been so excited at all the opportunities they would have. With six-month-old Tilly in tow, the future had looked so bright.

It was the long hours that had finally prompted them to look at Jez moving overseas. As a junior doctor in the busy London hospital where he worked, they had been seeing less and less of each other, and when Tilly had arrived, all helpless and dependent, Jez had found it too hard to be away from them both. So when an old friend of his from uni told him about the position at Mount Pleasant here in Hong Kong, it had seemed like a no-brainer. A forty-hour week, that was the deal breaker. Yes, of course the money and package were great, but a forty-hour week was what made him apply for the position immediately.

Six weeks later they had boarded the flight from Heathrow to Hong Kong with barely a second thought. They had packed their lives into four suitcases, putting anything they couldn't bring into storage for their return, whenever that might be. The initial contract was for twelve months but Jez hoped they would stay much longer.

They had settled in almost overnight.

The job came with accommodation, and theirs was a bright and airy apartment overlooking Victoria Park on Hong Kong Island. It was similar in size to the one they had left in Hampstead, but with its marble floors and modern fittings it had felt so much more luxurious. Three bedrooms, one was the guest room for now, but they both hoped for a brother or sister for little Tilly one day.

Perfect, life was perfect. The job at Mount Pleasant was awesome, so much more time to spend with his patients and he felt he could finally give the care he had trained to do, without the pressure that came from working in the underfunded NHS hospitals. Mount Pleasant was purely a private hospital, so most of the workers and patients were expats or tourists, and the language barrier hadn't been as much of a problem as he had worried.

Ness had settled quickly, joining the expat mother and baby groups, and soon formed a close group of friends bonded by their lives here. She had loved the convenience of Hong Kong. All the shops opened so late, and everything she could need, from baby milk to Chanel was on her doorstep. They had employed a maid, a lovely lady called Arinya from Thailand. At home a maid was a real luxury but here everyone seemed to have one. Ness was like a young girl again; not only was her husband around so much more but she didn't have the stress of mundane things like cooking and cleaning! She was happy with life, just another baby would make it even more perfect, and they were enjoying trying!

Jacob arrived almost exactly two years after Tilly, one day after her birthday on 31st July to be exact. It had been such a hot and humid summer in Hong Kong, and Ness had really struggled through her last trimester.

As she laid in her hospital bed in the maternity department of Mount Pleasant she had cradled her beautiful boy with his thick black hair. He looked exactly like Jez; now there were two gorgeous men in her life.

'Mummy!'

Tilly had hurtled into the room clutching a white polar bear teddy and climbed straight onto the bed.

'This is for the baby,' she exclaimed, all overexcited and giggling.

She thrust the teddy at Jacob.

'Here,' she said, expecting him to take it and probably say thank you too. Manners were very important to her!

'Let's lay him in the cot with it,' suggested Ness kindly. 'I'm sure he loves it, darling, but it will be a while before he can tell you.'

Tilly looked confused and disappointed; this baby was clearly not what she had hoped for at all!

Ness smiled at Jez, who was leaning against the doorway, beaming at them.

'I love you, Ness.'

'I should hope so,' she teased as she tucked Jacob and his bear into their cot and squeezed Tilly tight.

If only they had known then that Ness was already ill.

She had tried over the next week to breastfeed Jacob but it was just so painful. Mastitis, the doctor had presumed, and it seemed a logical explanation. But it wouldn't clear up, even after two courses of antibiotics, like it should have done, yet still they hadn't worried.

Further tests had ensued, and then they had received the devastating news.

'I'm very sorry to tell you that you have inflammatory breast cancer, Mrs Holland.'

The words didn't seem to make sense.

Cancer? No, she just had an infection in her milk ducts.

She looked up at Jez for help, to tell the doctor he was wrong, but he just looked back at her, helpless.

'We will start your treatment tomorrow, we have no time to waste.'

As they had sat there in that room after the doctor left, Jez holding Ness so close she could barely breathe, they both tried to process what they had just been told.

Why hadn't he known? He was a doctor, for God's sake, he should have seen it. Had she not just had the baby he might have known it was something more sinister, but mastitis was so common he too had presumed that was what it was.

'Presumption is the mother of all fuck-ups,' someone had once said to him, and this echoed loudly in his head.

Even the best doctors in Hong Kong and London couldn't save his beautiful Ness – the cancer had been too advanced. To watch his beautiful wife struggle to cope with the treatment, battling so bravely, had torn him to pieces inside. He should have been able to help her, but he couldn't. Less than a year after having Jacob she passed away in his arms. She had lost her fight and he had lost his heart and soul.

Over twelve months had passed now though, and while the pain was still there Jez was finally beginning to put back together the pieces of his life. He had to, for the sake of the children. The tears that had come every night came less frequently, and he even managed to smile when he remembered her now. He had had to forgive himself for not being able to save her, as the guilt had eaten away at him and he had found himself in a very dark place.

It was his mother Linda's gentle guidance that had pulled them all through. He was quite awestruck by her strength and wisdom, realising that he had never truly appreciated her until now. For years since his father had passed away he had wished she would find someone else to share her life with, but she had always insisted that she couldn't replace him. Only since he had lost Ness could he truly understand how she felt.

Chapter 4

Room 2301 at the Park Lane Hotel, Olivia's home for the next two days.

She propped her door open with her suitcase and quickly swept the room for hidden attackers. Whilst it was highly unlikely that anyone was hiding under the bed, in the wardrobe or behind the curtains, she always checked just as they had told her to in her training.

Fabulous. No rapists or murderers, she thought, half mocking herself. She closed the door now that her checks were done and gave a sigh of relief as she stepped out of her heels.

Her room on the twenty-third floor was luxurious, with its huge bed and its crisp white sheets. She walked towards the floor-to-ceiling windows and gazed in awe at the lights of Hong Kong. It was dark now and the city was lit up in all of its wonderful glory. Lights as far and as high as she could see, the colours and displays never failing to impress her. She opened the minibar and took out the small bottle of white wine. Pouring it into the wine glass she had just taken from the shelf above, she took out her phone and called Tom. It was almost midday at home, Hong Kong was eight hours ahead.

No answer.

Must be busy, she thought.

Tom was always busy lately. In the early days he was never too busy to take her calls. He ran his own building business so he worked long hours, but he would always drop everything to talk to her. Now she was lucky if she could get hold of him at all when she was away.

'Sorry babe, the business has gone crazy,' he said when she had complained. 'Anyway, we get plenty of time to talk when you are home.'

He was right, they had lived together for three years now and were together every evening, when she was home. But it was those days that she was away that she really missed him. He may have become so comfortable in their relationship that he didn't need to talk every day, but she hadn't yet. He was her best friend and she needed to tell him everything!

Must be a woman thing, she resigned herself. *Oh well.*

19:15, the clock said. Forty-five minutes until she had to meet the rest of the crew in the bar, better start getting ready!

Chapter 5

Ouch, ouch, OUCH!

Olivia's head throbbed as she opened one eye to see the light streaming through the gap in her curtains.

The night out had gone off in typical Hong Kong fashion. A few drinks in the hotel bar and then off to Lan Kwai Fong. Olivia loved it down there, with its cobbled hills lined with bars buzzing with people from all over the world. She vaguely recalled that they had ended up in Dusk Til Dawn, singing loudly along to the rock band on stage. Out of the corner of her eye she could see a pair of flashing bunny ears on the pillow next to her and she giggled to herself. A night in Hong Kong wouldn't be complete if you didn't buy something that flashed from one of the numerous vendors that sold their wares around the bars.

Sitting herself up slowly, she looked around for her handbag. Finding it by the side of her bed, she rummaged through for some painkillers.

Sorry I missed your call babe, hope you had a good flight. A message from Tom on her mobile.

Fine thanks, night out was better! Awful hangover now though, she replied, and she wasn't lying.

Coffee, that's what she needed now.

She threw on some clothes and headed out. It was nearly 4pm and the city was starting to cool down. Olivia liked to stay partially on UK time whilst she was here, it helped with the jet lag when she got home, and so sleeping in until the afternoon wasn't unusual for her. It was too hot to go out in the day at this time of year anyway; the humidity could be unbearable.

As she walked back from the coffee shop to the hotel she glanced across the road to the park. *A nice walk will clear my head*, she thought as she crossed over.

Victoria Park was like a calm oasis in the middle of the skyscrapers and the craziness of the city around it. A statue of Queen Victoria greeted her as she entered and Olivia gave her a cursory nod as she passed. She walked along the path that snaked around its perimeter, drinking in the smells and noises that scratched away at her senses, watching the people go about their lives around her. The children playing, the cute little old Chinese couples walking hand-in-hand, the man on the bench with his bird in a beautiful wicker cage, the small fluffy dogs that barked excitedly at each other.

Eventually she stopped at a bench underneath a huge old fir tree, sitting down to finish her coffee. There was a children's play area just opposite and their happy voices hung in the air around her like beautiful wind chimes. Olivia really did love her job for giving her moments like this.

'Happy birthday to you, happy birthday to you.'

English voices.

'Happy birthday dear Tilly and Jacob, happy birthday to you.'

Aww, a children's birthday party, how sweet.

She stood up to make a move back to the hotel, glancing over to where the singing was coming from. About a dozen children were all sat in a circle on a red blanket, the remains of a tea party scattered around them. The two birthday children were both leaning over a big chocolate cake at the far end, blowing out the candles.

'Smile, you two.'

A man with a camera was standing just in front of Olivia. He looked vaguely familiar but she could only see his back so it was hard to tell.

'Over here, look at Daddy,' he called, waving his hand in the air.

Click went the camera.

'Get in the photo, Mother.'

A blonde lady walked over and smiled at the camera, an arm around each child.

Oh!

Suddenly Olivia realised who it was. Of all the places in Hong Kong they were here, the family from the plane! That meant the man with the camera…

Ping. A text message on her phone. She pulled it

out of her bag.

Call me when you get a minute. Love Mum xxx

She looked back up, and he was looking straight at her, quizzically.

'Hi.' He sounded unsure.

'Oh, hi,' she replied. Why did she feel embarrassed suddenly? Perhaps because he was even more attractive now than he had been on the plane, and she worried that the admiration may show on her face?

'It is you! I thought it was! Fancy seeing you here!' The penny had obviously dropped and he looked genuinely pleased to see her.

'My hotel is just there.' She gestured in the direction of The Park Lane, unable to think of anything more poignant to say.

'Well what a small world, I live just next to you,' he replied, and pointed to a high-rise building not far from her hotel.

'Oh,' Olivia replied, still struggling with what to say.

'Daddy, Daddy,' a small voice called, and Tilly bounded over, grabbing hold of her father's trousers, 'we are going to start the games.'

She looked at Olivia.

'Do you remember the nice lady from the airplane, darling?' he asked his daughter.

The little girl looked at Olivia and studied her for a moment.

'I think so,' she said sweetly.

To be fair, thought Olivia, *I do look quite different*

onboard than I do right now. For a moment she wished she had made a little bit of an effort before leaving her room, but she really hadn't expected to run into anyone she knew or might have to talk to!

'I'm sorry, please forgive me, I don't even know your name.'

'Olivia.'

'Jez, and this is Tilly, and that little terror over there is Jacob.' He gestured over to his son, who had just smothered his whole face in chocolate cake.

'Will you come and play games with us?' asked Tilly.

Olivia opened her mouth to excuse herself.

'Pleeeeeeease.'

She looked at the sweet little girl pleading with her and then at Jez.

'Olivia, we would love you to join us.'

How could she refuse?

Five minutes later Olivia found herself blindfolded and surrounded by giggling children. Tilly had obviously known that Olivia, as the new arrival, would have to do her beckoning, and was taking full advantage. She felt slightly ridiculous as she reached out around her, trying to grab hold of absolutely anyone, so that she could end her turn as quickly as possible. Where were they?!

At last, a body!

She grabbed the arm tight, but it wasn't a child's arm, it was muscular and warm. She held on probably a moment more than she should have done.

'You got me!' Jez said softly.

Olivia jumped and let go as if she had been burned. Her cheeks flushed and her heart raced. Of all the people to catch! She hoped he wouldn't notice her blushing.

'Sorry,' she said, taking off her blindfold hastily and handing it to him. 'Your turn.'

The games continued for at least the next hour. Piñata, pass the parcel, all the classics. Olivia genuinely loved children and found Tilly and Jacob absolutely adorable. They clearly loved Olivia too, both vying for her attention and Tilly insisting that she take part in everything!

Chapter 6

'Champagne?'

It was Linda, standing there with a bottle of Bollinger and a stack of plastic cups. She smiled at Olivia and offered her a cup, filling it with champagne.

'Sorry about the cups but we couldn't risk glass out here.'

'No, of course not,' agreed Olivia.

'It's so lovely of you to join us, Olivia, it's really made Tilly's day,' said Linda warmly. 'It was meant to be that we bumped into you today.'

'Thank you, you're too kind,' replied Olivia. 'Thank you for letting me join you, I've loved it so much.' She really had.

The sun was beginning to set and slowly the parents started to gather up their children and say their goodbyes. Olivia probably should have left then too but she didn't really want to; she was loving the ease of being with Jez and his family. Tilly had a wisdom as if she had been here before in another life, and entertained Olivia with her observations and analogies. Jacob was just a bundle of cuteness, and Linda was the perfect host, mother and grandmother. She was intrigued by Olivia's job and lifestyle, quizzing her on destinations and layovers. In return she opened up to her about how she had come to be in Hong Kong with her family, and Olivia warmed to them all even more.

'I really must get these two babies home,' she said suddenly, realising it was now dark and Jacob was slumbering already in his stroller.

Olivia was just about to say her goodbyes when Jez looked at her and held up a bottle of champagne he had just opened.

'Will you stay here and finish this with me, Olivia?' he asked, tilting his head and raising his eyebrows.

How could she refuse? Not only was she an absolute sucker for champagne but she was enjoying his company, maybe a little bit too much.

They sat on the bench talking for another hour, not about Ness, this wasn't the time, and Olivia inexplicably couldn't bring herself to mention Tom. They talked about their jobs, their childhoods, and their mutual love of Hong Kong.

The champagne had given her a warm and contented feeling and she closed her eyes briefly to take in the sounds and smells around her. As she did so Jez leaned in and kissed her so gently on the lips that she barely felt it, but it was definitely there. She opened her eyes and stared straight into his, losing herself in the moment.

She should have pushed him away, or told him to stop, but instead she received him willingly as he leaned back in towards her and their lips met again, lingering this time, gently caressing. He stroked her long dark hair, running his fingers gently down her face and along her neck, giving her goosebumps despite the heat of the night. Afterwards they sat on the bench in silence, him holding her tightly in his strong arms. Olivia felt the warmth of his body and his heart beating, it was racing just like hers was.

She hadn't been close to another man since she had met Tom. This moment wasn't real, she told herself, she had just got carried away with the atmosphere and the champagne, yet she found it so hard to break away.

'I have to go,' she said eventually, pulling herself up and looking sadly at him.

'Ok.' It was as if he too knew that this was only a moment in time, not the beginning of something, and they walked in silence, arm in arm, back to the park's entrance. He hugged her goodbye, kissing her one last time, and she felt him watching her as she walked back towards her hotel. She never turned around, never looked back.

Chapter 7

Olivia stared out of the window as the aircraft took off. She heard the landing gear going up and the whir of hydraulics as the pilots adjusted the rudder to steer the plane in the direction of home. Hong Kong twinkled below them, the millions of lights starting to blur into one as they climbed higher.

She remembered the events of the night before in every beautiful detail, shuddering as she recalled the way his touch had made her feel. She could still imagine the strength of his arms around her and smell him as if he was sat right there next to her. She fought the feelings of guilt that kept trying to ruin the memories; she would come back to them later, but while she could still see Hong Kong she wanted to stay in that moment as long as she possibly could.

The flight back to London was over an hour longer than coming out, but it felt like infinitely more. It would have helped if she had been able to sleep on her break but her thoughts kept her awake. As they had got closer to home she had had to put the memories in a box, fasten the lid tight, and store them away safely at the back of her mind. It had been a kiss, that was all, a moment of madness thousands of miles away and she couldn't let that one moment affect her real life, the one she shared with Tom.

It was five years and seven months to be exact since she had been introduced to Tom by her friend Lindsey. She and Lindsey had been friends since school, and while Olivia had wanted to travel and see the world, Lin had settled down to life in the country with her husband Pete and her greatest love, her horses. Whilst they were busy raising their two children and living their dream, Olivia was having a string of failed relationships with the wrong men.

Her lifestyle meant that she met people from walks of life that she wasn't really part of. Her mother had single-handedly raised her, and her sister Shelley, working long hours at a local supermarket to give them a warm home and the things they needed after their father had left when they were small. The places Olivia went now meant meeting people that came mostly from a different background and that was generally where the relationships would fail. Despite dressing in nice clothes now and living what some people would deem a glamorous life, Olivia was still that working-class girl at heart and put little importance on material things. Most of the men she met, however, seemed to think money bought them entitlement, and the right to be judgemental of others. How could she take them to her mum's tiny apartment, or introduce them to people who still lived her old life? While she could dress appropriately and fit into their circles, it never seemed so easy to do the other way around. Either they could not accept or respect her loved ones, or she was unable to bring herself to tell them about her background. There would inevitably come a time when their differences would become too much and moving forward to a committed relationship was just too difficult, needing too much compromise.

Tom was different to them. He and Pete had worked together for years and Lindsey had known he was perfect for her friend. When she had introduced them at her New Year's Eve party the chemistry had been instant.

Tom was tall and strong, and a couple of years older than her – just how Olivia liked her men. She hadn't been able to stop herself looking at the curves of his biceps through the sleeves which stretched over them, and the pull of his shirt over his chest hinted at the muscles beneath it. He had been dressed immaculately in expensive clothes, and smelt so good that she had found herself standing closer than was really necessary to him, just so that she could breathe in his aroma.

His dark hair was cropped close to his head and whilst he was closely shaven, that night he wore at least a day's worth of stubble. It was his smile that she had loved the most though, crinkling right up to the corners of his beautiful deep green eyes, which seemed to look straight into her soul. Despite oozing confidence and success, when he spoke to her he was so humble and kind, and oh so funny!

They were inseparable for the rest of the night, and as she had stared into his eyes when he had first kissed her she had known he was the one she wanted to be with for the rest of her life, something she had always believed was a myth until that moment.

Tom, like Olivia, had grown up in a working-class family but had worked hard and slowly built up his building company. It was his true passion, after her of course, she would tease him. As their relationship blossomed they spoke about marriage and children often, but he just wanted to get them in the best position possible first, and she admired his focus, forever wanting to climb higher. There was no rush anyhow, she would tell herself, they were committed completely to each other and that was enough for her, for now. They had moved into a beautiful new house in Kent last year and she had to admit she was enjoying the fruits of his labour. Of course she wished he wasn't always so busy but she had to accept he was doing it for them and their future and she loved him even more for it.

As she sat on her jumpseat flicking through memories and thoughts of Tom in her mind, she tried to understand why she had fallen for Jez, when she already had everything she could possibly want. She had obviously just got too comfortable in their relationship and forgotten, for that moment, that she had everything already. It wouldn't happen again.

As the plane's wheels touched down at Heathrow Olivia took out her phone and switched it on. Tom's gorgeous face smiled back at her on her home screen.

Can't wait to see you, will be keeping the bed warm ;). He had sent the message last night whilst she was flying.

Oh yes, it was Sunday. Tom was home, she realised, and felt herself getting excited. Back to reality on this beautiful sunny Sunday morning.

Chapter 8

Olivia drove her Mercedes out of the Heathrow staff car park and headed towards the M25. The sun was shining, music blared from her speakers and she was looking forward to climbing into bed with her man. A picture of Jez popped into her mind but she pushed it straight back. Why had she been so silly? Maybe she had needed to be reminded, it was natural after so many years that they would take each other for granted a little, wasn't it?

Suddenly she remembered the message from her mum to call her. She checked her watch; it was 7am but Mum would be up by now, perhaps talking to her would take her mind off things.

'Siri, call Mum,' she instructed, and the ring tone started to play over the Bluetooth.

'Hi Mum, sorry I forgot to call you back Friday,' she apologised.

'That's ok darling, I just hadn't heard from you for a while.'

'Sorry, I've just been so busy with minimum rest between flights, it's always manic in the summer months.' She wasn't exaggerating either, these last few weeks had been really full-on. 'I've just got back from Hong Kong now though, so we can have a good catch up while I drive home. You can keep me awake.'

'Glad to help out.' She knew her mum was pleased at the opportunity, always desperate for a good natter.

They caught up on the family news, how cousin Paula was pregnant again with her fifth child, and that her husband Dave was going to have a vasectomy now. Apparently Mum's brother Shane had been arrested for fighting again and his wife was in pieces; the poor thing suffered with her nerves as it was. Olivia may live a different life now but they were all still her family and she would never forget her roots, their lives were just a little dramatic for her sometimes, she thought. It passed her journey home though and it was nice to hear her mum sounding so animated. She should call her for a chat more often.

As she hung up the call she pulled into her road in Edenbridge. Their house was a little way up on the right, behind tall wooden gates that Tom had installed himself in the brick wall that separated them from the street. She clicked the button on the remote control on the dashboard and they opened slowly to welcome her back. The house wasn't huge but it was no means small either. Detached and set over three storeys, it was probably too big for just the two of them, but they would fill it with children one day, and for now they often had visitors. Tom had converted the whole basement into a den with a bar and dancefloor so they could entertain their friends, and they had a pretty good social life as a result.

She pulled her car in front of the second garage door next to Tom's Audi, switched off the engine and jumped out. She would come back for her case later but right now she didn't just want but *needed* to see Tom.

She crept quietly into the house and up to their bedroom. He hadn't heard her coming from their bedroom at the back of their house. She stood at the door and watched him dozing, the daylight bathing him in golden rays. She hadn't looked at him properly for such a long time and had forgotten how beautiful he was. His arms were outside of the covers and her need to be in them was overwhelming. She undressed right there in the doorway and climbed naked into the bed. Tom opened his eyes and gave her a sleepy smile as he wrapped her up and made love to her.

'I love you, Tom,' she breathed, and had never meant it more.

Chapter 9

Olivia awoke to the sound of the radio blaring downstairs, Tom singing out of tune to the song that was playing and banging around loudly in the kitchen. She glanced at the clock on the bedside table, 12:05. The sun was still shining and she didn't want to waste this glorious day, getting up and showering quickly in the en-suite bathroom.

'We've been invited to a barbecue over at James and Sam's,' Tom called through the bathroom door.

'Perfect.' Olivia switched off the water and opened the shower door. He passed her a towel and she began to dry herself off. 'What time?'

'Not until two,' he watched her wipe the water from her face and grinned cheekily at her whilst looking her up and down, 'so I think I'll just take you back to bed for a while,' and before Olivia could disagree he had swept her up as if she weighed nothing and carried her back through to the bedroom. Their love life hadn't been this good for ages. Tom was always tired lately, but Olivia wasn't complaining and relished every second of his attentions. She should land back on Sunday mornings more often, she through wryly.

The barbecue was in full swing when they arrived, with probably about thirty or forty people gathered in small groups around James and Sam's perfectly manicured lawn. Sam emerged from the summer house at the bottom carrying a tray of glasses of Pimm's, all garnished beautifully with fruit and screaming 'summer'. She worked her way towards them, weaving in and out of the small children that were running around.

'So glad you two could make it,' she exclaimed loudly as she came closer. 'Olivia, Tom says you've just landed from Hong Kong, you must be exhausted!'

'Oh I'm fine, Sam, I just had a few hours' sleep, I couldn't miss seeing you all!' She reached forward and pecked Sam on the cheek affectionately.

'Well if you get tired just climb into a spare bed, you know where they are.' They had stayed over here many times rather than drive home after a few drinks. It was nice to know she could sneak off later if she needed to, but Tom had work in the morning so it probably wouldn't be a late one. 'James is around here somewhere.' She looked around the garden. 'He's probably getting some bits for the barbecue. Let me go and put this tray down, be back in a minute.'

Olivia took a glass of Pimm's and Sam sashayed away with her tray. Tom was deep in conversation already with a man she had never seen before about football, and as much as Olivia wanted to share everything with him, sport just wasn't her thing. She scanned the garden looking for someone more interesting to talk to.

'I'm just going to talk to Sam's mum,' she said, and touched him on the arm, but was unsure if he had heard her. He would talk about football for hours so probably wouldn't even notice she'd gone!

She headed over to where Sam's mother Janet was sat at a table under a large umbrella. She was with Sam's sister Fiona and a younger girl that she didn't recognise.

'Hello,' she said cheerily and greeted each of them individually with an embrace. 'Hi, I'm Olivia,' she introduced herself to the girl that she didn't know and held out her hand informally.

'Olivia, this is Sarah,' introduced Fiona.

Sarah stood up quickly and shook her hand eagerly. 'Hi, pleased to meet you!' she exclaimed in a strong Australian accent.

'Sarah is an old school friend of mine's niece,' explained Fiona. 'She wanted to come and try living in the UK so she's staying with us and helping with the kids until she finds something more permanent.'

'Oh fantastic, how exciting for you!' Olivia loved to see people travel and explore the world, especially while they were young like Sarah. She had always found people who didn't want to travel so frustrating, they had no idea how amazing the world was out there She wanted everyone to see all of the fascinating places she had seen. 'How long are you staying for?'

'At least a year, but maybe longer if I find

something, or someone, worth staying for,' she giggled, looking around.

'I am sure you will.' And she meant it, as this girl was beautiful in the beach babe way that was rare around here. Long tanned and toned limbs poked out of her cute playsuit that hugged her slim figure, and her hair tumbled in naturally bleached waves around her shoulders. There was no doubt the single young men would be falling over each other for this girl's attentions!

'Have you been anywhere nice lately Olivia?' asked Janet.

'I landed back from Hong Kong just this morning Janet,' she replied.

'*Awesome*,' Sarah cut in. 'What do you do?'

'Oh, I'm a flight attendant.'

'Wow! I'd love to do that! That must be the best job in the world!'

'I like it, yes, but it's not for everyone.' Not everyone could cope with the lack of sleep and being away from home, it was true. Olivia started to tell her about the ups and downs of life as a flight attendant, about the less glamorous routes and sheer hard work that came as part of the job. Sarah listened intently to begin with but suddenly seemed to become distracted. She kept looking over Olivia's shoulder at something and had started flicking her hair around and giggling at the wrong times to Olivia's stories. Oh! She had obviously spotted someone she liked, realised Olivia, and she wrapped up her speech sharply, Sarah not even noticing the half-finished tale.

Whoever it was that had got Sarah's attention was getting closer; this girl was so obvious Olivia was a little embarrassed for her. Then just as Olivia felt an arm around her shoulder a brief look of confusion flashed across her face.

'There you are.' Tom kissed her forehead. 'I wondered where you'd gone.'

Oh my word, she'd fancied *her* Tom! Olivia tried not to laugh. Yes, she knew he was a good-looking guy but this girl couldn't have been much older than twenty, and Tom would never be interested in her, even with her youthful beauty. She trusted him implicitly.

'Tom this is Sarah, Sarah this is my partner Tom.'

'Pleased to meet you, Sarah.'

Olivia looked at her expecting to see a flash of embarrassment, or at least disappointment, but there was none.

'Likewise, Tom.' She smiled at him as if auditioning for a toothpaste advert, and fluttered her eyelashes much more than was necessary. Was she *flirting*? Oh my word, this girl was bold! Olivia had always prided herself on not being a jealous type but this girl's audacity was more than mildly annoying. 'Olivia was just telling me about her job, you must really miss her when she's away.' Was she hoping he would say that he didn't?! *Tom had better give the right answer here,* Olivia thought.

'Of course,' he grinned. 'Excuse me, ladies, I'm just going to lend a hand.' He kissed Olivia again and headed off after James who had just walked past with a huge tray of meat for the barbecue.

They both stood there for a moment in silence. Olivia didn't know what to say now and Sarah had just watched Tom walk away admiringly, as if she was oblivious to the fact he was Olivia's partner.

'Lucky you,' Sarah remarked, looking back at Olivia. 'Your boyfriend is hot!'

'Thanks, I know.' She couldn't disguise the warning tone in her voice, and knew that her smile wasn't quite reaching her eyes. Olivia wrestled with her emotions; she knew she was probably being oversensitive, it was landing day after all and she was tired. She supposed she was actually complimenting her in a roundabout way. The girl was just young and excitable, she would find herself a suitable muse soon enough. 'Nice to meet you, Sarah, I'd better go and help them before the burgers get cremated.'

'Nice to meet you too, Olivia,' she said genuinely and turned back towards the table where Fiona was sitting.

Chapter 10

As the afternoon unwound and the Pimm's took effect Olivia relaxed and floated between people, chatting easily and enjoying the atmosphere. Summertime music played over the garden speakers and the food and drinks flowed endlessly, the aromas from the barbecue filling the air. As she moved from one group of familiar faces to another she told animated stories of her latest travels; people were always so keen to hear about her adventures. Of course, she might have used some creativity with some, no one wanted to hear she hadn't left her hotel room in New York, or that she had run out of chicken on the flight home. Others she held back on, like what had really happened in the park in Hong Kong.

There it was again, out of its box in her mind, an image of Jez popped into her head and caught her completely by surprise. Suddenly she felt guilty, or that's what she supposed that feeling in the pit of her stomach was, and she forced the thoughts away.

There was nothing to be gained by thinking about any of that, she told herself firmly.

Before she had realised it, she found herself standing face-to-face with Sarah again, but any animosity she had felt earlier had gone now and she was almost pleased to have a second chance to befriend the girl. Olivia was uncomfortable with bad feelings and always looked to find the best in people. Sometimes it could make her seem a little naive but she preferred to be like that rather than unkind and judgemental. She had learned that being kind to people made her feel much nicer than the alternative.

'Hello again, Sarah.' She smiled her friendliest smile.

'Hi Olivia,' still full of excitement and energy.

'Are you having a nice time?'

'Yes thanks, I've met some really lovely people.'

'So do you think you will like it here? Don't you miss your friends and family at home?' Olivia couldn't imagine moving so far away from those that she loved.

'A little I guess but I was home schooled when I was a kid so I don't have loads of good friends. I'm excited to make new ones here. Everyone has been so lovely to me so far.'

'And what about work? Do you like looking after Fiona's children?'

'Oh they're adorable, I love them so much, but I need to find another job and get some money soon. I want to visit Europe while I'm so close, I can't wait to see Paris and Rome, and Berlin. There are so many places I need to go to.'

'Well it would be a shame not to.' Olivia was starting to really like this girl's energy and wondered how she could help her achieve her dreams. Suddenly it dawned on her, just as Tom walked towards them.

'Hello ladies. Sorry I've left you on your own so long, babe.' He draped his arm around Olivia and nodded a greeting at Sarah.

'No worries, I've been having a lovely time. Tom, Sarah's looking for some work, weren't you looking for someone to cover for Kiera?' She remembered him saying a while ago that his receptionist was due to go on maternity leave soon, but he had been too busy to organise anyone to cover her.

He looked at Olivia and then at Sarah, but he seemed a little unsure, and Olivia suddenly felt bad for putting him on the spot.

'Have you got any experience in building, Sarah?' he asked doubtfully.

'Actually, I do!' Tom looked surprised, as was Olivia. 'My father has a building company back in Oz and I've helped him out plenty, I can lay a damn good brick wall!'

Olivia and Tom both stood there speechless with their mouths open. This girl had just completely shocked them both. It was Tom who broke the silence when he laughed.

'Well that was not what I expected.' The girls both laughed along with him. 'When can you start?'

By the time they left the barbecue later that evening Sarah had secured herself the job and was due to come in the following week to shadow Keira before she left. Olivia hadn't forgotten that Sarah thought her boyfriend was hot but didn't find her threatening now, and she was pleased with herself for being such a nice person, and for helping the young girl out.

As she fell asleep in Tom's arms that night she had no doubt about his feelings, and knew that she didn't need to worry about him being distracted by anyone else; he only had eyes for her. But wasn't that what he had thought about her, and she had been distracted, hadn't she? She hoped the memories of Hong Kong would fade soon as they were tainting her perfect world.

Chapter 11

Olivia's three days off passed quickly as always, and by Wednesday night she was sat on her bedroom floor, surrounded by clothes and toiletries, packing her suitcase again.

'I wish you weren't going for so long,' Tom complained as he watched her from the bed.

'Me too,' she lied, trying to look sad. Whereas usually she would feel the same, she couldn't help being excited for this trip.

Bikinis, sun tan lotion, summer dresses, check!

She would need little else in Jamaica, and that was where she would be for the next four days and nights, with Claire, one of her closest friends, and Nicola and Ali. She and Claire had been friends since way before joining the airline and now that they lived on opposite sides of town, it was sometimes easier to get quality time together at work than at home. Claire, like so many other crew, had been unlucky in love. Despite being absolutely stunning with long chestnut hair and a model's figure, and having the kindest heart of anyone else Olivia knew, she just couldn't find a decent man. She had recently arrived home from a flight to find her latest beau in bed with another woman, and the one before that had been having an affair too. It was worrying how often Olivia had heard such stories from other crew members, how it only took a miscommunication about which day or what time they were landing for them to be caught out. Good job she trusted Tom as it was almost too easy for these men to lead double lives when the girls were away at work.

She could barely remember the flights that they had flown with Nicola and Ali that had cemented those friendships, but it was funny how you could simply click with some people and want them in your life. Nicola, with her English rose features and flame-red hair, and Ali the little 'pocket rocket' as she heard someone once call her, all blonde and curvy and so petite she could only just close the hat racks.

They had all used their monthly bid to request this trip as it was Claire's birthday. Why settle for a night out at home when they could have four nights in Jamaica?! The downside was that they would have to work the flight, and these were notoriously hard, but it was a small price to pay for the treat they would get when they arrived.

It was a welcome surprise when they arrived at the briefing room to find that Julie Margot was the manager on this flight too, since it was unusual to fly with the same crewmember two flights in a row. As the rest of the crew came in and took their seats she began to brief them on the aircraft and the flight.

'We are on a Boeing 747-400, and unfortunately we are full to the brim today.'

Everyone groaned.

'But with this lovely crew we can't possibly have a bad day so let's just try to enjoy it. Work hard, be nice to the passengers and we will be on that beach with a rum punch in the blink of an eye.'

Her positivity radiated across the room and the rest of the crew, fourteen of them altogether, all hoping that she was right!

'We do have three deportees who are all escorted…'

I hope they are well behaved, thought Olivia. Some deportees were fine, being sent home for simply having the wrong paperwork or overstaying their visas, but these types were seldom escorted by guards. The ones that were escorted were usually prisoners who had finished their sentences and may have committed awful crimes, and most of them really didn't want to go home.

Julie continued with a safety briefing, reminding them of the safety features of the aircraft and procedures they would follow in an emergency, and then they all left the room together and started to make their way to the aircraft.

'I so need this break,' Claire said as they walked side by side. 'I can't wait to spend time with my besties.'

'Just gotta survive the flight first, hey?' said Olivia, pulling a tortured face.

Chapter 12

Olivia and Claire stood at the aircraft door as the three prisoners shuffled down to the back of the aircraft. Handcuffed and swamped by guards, they didn't protest too loudly and were soon firmly placed into their seats. No dramas were to be had today by the looks of things, that was a relief, sometimes they could really make a fuss. The rest of the passengers followed slowly after, with their abundance of hand luggage and lack of patience. The crew were soon busy sorting out seating problems and offloading bags to the hold. It was always a mystery how they made it to the departure gate with far more hand luggage than they were allowed, and on a full flight there certainly wasn't room to store it all in the cabin.

'Well good morning ladies and gentlemen, and a very warm welcome onboard this Osprey Aviation flight OS657 to Montego Bay…' And so it began.

It was never going to be an easy flight, these never were, but this flight was exceptional! At the point at which they ran out of chicken meals with ten rows still to serve you would have thought they had run out of fuel by the shock and horror it caused amongst the passengers!

'We want chicken, we want chicken,' chanted the Jamaican lady in 53D, whilst banging her fists on her table.

'We want chicken,' joined in the passengers around her.

Olivia looked across to Claire and Ali who were on the cart in the opposite aisle and couldn't help but laugh at the ridiculousness of the situation.

'Ladies, please, if I could find any more chickens I would catch them and cook them for you myself!'

The ladies stopped their chant, realising the futility of their protest and found the funny side as the girls had done.

'Now would you like the beef or the pasta?' Olivia offered, trying not to sound too much like a school teacher scolding her children.

As she got to the rear of the aircraft she checked that the guards were all ok, and felt a tinge of sympathy when she saw the look of sadness on the face of one of the prisoners. *How do people's lives go so wrong when we are all brought into the world equal?* she thought. When she and Tom had a child they would make sure it had all the best opportunities in life and they would guide them to be a good person and to always do the right things. Perhaps if these men had had a better start they wouldn't have ended up here now, like this. The other prisoner on her side of the aircraft didn't evoke the same sympathy, as he glared at her with dead eyes, and Olivia put down his dinner tray without a word and quickly moved on.

Apart from a brief hour-long break they didn't stop all flight, and by the time the seatbelt signs came on for landing they all sank exhausted into their jumpseats, welcoming the excuse to sit down and not have to answer any more call bells!

The flight had passed in a flash, just as Julie had promised, and now for the good bit.

As their bus pulled through the gate of the Sun Palace they all looked toward the bright blue sea that glistened in the sunshine straight ahead. The colonial-style main building stood proudly on the left, all whitewashed with its huge arched opening showing off its magnificent interior. A smartly uniformed man stood at the central table to greet them, with the promised rum punches poured ready. They couldn't get off the bus quick enough, heading straight to him as the bus driver unloaded their bags.

'Cheers,' exclaimed Nicola, raising her glass triumphantly.

'Cheers,' replied the others in unison, raising their own and forgetting the stresses of the flight with their first sips of the local poison.

'My room, 344, in an hour for bubbles, girls,' called Julie as she glided past them moments later, a bellman following her dutifully, carrying her bags. Olivia doubted that they would all have the luxury of a personal attendant, but was not in the least bit surprised that Julie did.

'Is that an order?' laughed Claire.

'Think so,' said Nicola, equally amused by Julie's parting comment and demeanour.

'Well we had better get to our rooms and get ready then!' Olivia declared, finishing her drink.

Chapter 13

Lying on her sun lounger the next morning, Olivia breathed in the fresh sea air and listened to the rhythmic sounds of the sea. Ali relaxed next to her reading her book and soaking up the first of the days rays. The others would be along shortly; they had gone to play tennis, but she and Ali hadn't felt up to it this morning after the room party the night before.

She watched the two young children playing on the sand. The waves gently glided back and forth, just wetting their feet before retreating again. Several people were in the sea and she could hear their conversations if she listened hard enough, but she preferred to imagine what they were talking about as it was always much more interesting when she made it up.

She had seen the older couple that were treading water in the distance in the hotel bar the night before. They were clearly wealthy, the lady's jewellery sparkled too much to be anything but real diamonds, and she had the tell-tale signs of a face that was fighting the ageing process. As for the man, his choice of white linen trousers and tailored shirt on a slim body that belied his years, was something no man without a tan and perfect teeth like his could pull off, and it suited him perfectly.

She imagined they were called Barbie and Ken and that they were oil billionaires from Texas.

'Shall we go to the yacht to Cannes next week, Ken?'

'Why sure, Sugar, we'll take the Gulfstream over, I'll get Jackson to book it in.'

Olivia was so caught up in the imaginary conversation she didn't hear the other girls arrive. They were all hot from playing tennis and eagerly undressed down to their bikinis before dashing to the sea.

'C'mon Olivia,' called Claire over her shoulder.

Olivia put down her phone which she had been holding idly, and covered it with a towel before joining them for a swim. The sea was almost warm, although it still took her breath as it passed her waist as she walked in. Ali joined them a few minutes later with a glass of champagne for each of them and they toasted Claire's birthday, whilst marvelling at their surroundings and laughing about the night before.

'I'm sure Julie and the captain were getting together,' speculated Nicola.

'Oh my god, me too!' agreed Olivia.

'Did you see how close he was to her?'

'I know!'

'Was he still there when you left, Ali?' Ali had been the last one of their group to leave.

'Yep, but there were still a couple of the others there too.'

Olivia loved a bit of speculation, it was just harmless fun and provided amusement.

As she dried herself off and lay back on her sun lounger she noticed a notification on her phone's screen.

Sarah Fischer has sent a friend request.

Who? She couldn't think who Sarah Fischer was, and mentally tried to recall the names of the rest of the crew, thinking that it may be one of them. She opened the app and selected the notification. A picture of the Australian girl from the barbecue smiled back at her.

'Oh!' Olivia hadn't meant to say this out loud but her obvious surprise had made Claire look over at her questioningly.

'What's up, babe?'

'Oh, um, nothing!' she replied unconvincingly. She had almost forgotten about the girl, although Tom had mentioned something about her starting at the office soon. Something urged her to look at her profile and she found herself scrolling down through pictures of Sarah's life. Only there weren't really pictures of her life, just pictures of her. Where were her friends? She looked at one staged selfie after another, finally coming across one of her with her parents.

Happy Birthday darling, love Mum and Dad, it said. March 12th. A few obligatory Happy Birthdays followed, but none of any substance. More selfies and poses.

'Who's that?' asked Claire, who was now sat on the end of her lounger looking at her phone with her.

'Oh, a girl we met Sunday, friend of a friend. She's going to be working for Tom.'

'Oh, are you sure that's a good idea?' She looked concerned.

It was funny, she couldn't put her finger on why this girl's profile made her uneasy, but Claire saw it too. There was nothing to tell you anything about her, just that she had parents, but where were all her friends?? Her nights out? Holidays? Just one beautiful and posed photo after another, as if she thought that should be enough information for you.

She looked at her friends list; there were a few, not that they seemed to converse, only to say happy birthday, but that meant nothing about the depth of friendship.

1 mutual friend, it said – Tom. The unease in her stomach made her feel strange.

Well at least she could monitor her on here, she thought. She tried to brush off Claire's concern, it was probably borne from her own experiences, and she had no reason to feel worried. It was just a profile, maybe she didn't like posting much about her life. Some people were just private like that, weren't they?

'Champagne.' Ali arrived back from the bar with more glasses and Olivia put down her phone. Nothing would be gained from thinking too much about that.

Chapter 14

As she sunbathed that day Olivia couldn't help thinking about Sarah, picturing the girl in the photos installed in Tom's office, flirting with every man who walked through the door, including him. Whilst she was enjoying her time away with the girls the niggling thoughts in the back of her mind just wouldn't go away. She was sure, well almost, that she could trust Tom; he would never be tempted by someone like Sarah, would he? It would be better if she was just a brainless airhead though, and not one that could lay a brick wall! She had never felt insecure before, always confident enough in herself to know she was enough for him, and she just couldn't understand why she felt like this now. Then it hit her, it was because of what had happened in Hong Kong. As she had heard that daytime TV host say so many times, people who cheat are distrustful of their partners. Sure, it had only been a kiss, but she had been tempted by another man, why wouldn't Tom be tempted by another girl? If this worry and paranoia was a result of what she had done then maybe she deserved it. It was her punishment, she concluded. She had to let it go and stop judging Tom because of her own mistake; he hadn't done anything to deserve it, but maybe she would just have to keep an eye on Sarah.

'Pier One tonight, girls?' Julie Margot stood between them and the sea. She wore a white swimsuit, cut out at the sides, and a sun hat with a huge brim, immaculate as always. 'It's karaoke!' she exclaimed excitedly.

Olivia looked at the others, all woken from their daydreams and reading and looking at Julie as if she had just landed from Mars.

'Umm,' managed Nicola.

Claire looked at Olivia, horrified, and said nothing.

'Ooh, yes, I love karaoke.' And that was it, Ali had just committed them all to a night of The Julie Show. Olivia hated karaoke at the best of times, but karaoke with Julie Margot was seriously something else. She remembered Tokyo a few years back when Julie had pretty much hogged the mic all night thinking she was Whitney Houston, but she couldn't hold a note. She really hoped she had got better since then. Bloody Ali and her big mouth, she had obviously had too much champagne!

'Oh Ali, you have no idea what you've just signed us up to,' groaned Claire once Julie was out of hearing distance. She, too, knew of Julie's karaoke reputation.

'What?' Ali really did have no idea.

'You'll see tonight,' smirked Olivia. They were going now so had best just make the most of it.

Pier One was a restaurant situated, as its name suggested, on a pier down in Montego Bay. A grand square bar was positioned in the middle with tables all around the edges near to the water. Fairy lights twinkled along either side, reflecting in the sea below them, and the mandatory Bob Marley music played softly over the speakers. The crew all sat around a long table on the right-hand side looking out over the small boats that bobbed about in the marina in the inky darkness.

Frozen margaritas were flowing and everyone chatted animatedly amongst themselves. It was a strange thing to people who weren't crew how people who had never met before, or barely knew each other, could talk about every minute detail of their lives. Olivia always thought of it as crew counselling, they were all as good at listening as talking, and somebody would always have had a similar situation, or a worse problem before, and be able to give advice.

She found herself sat between Claire and Luke, who had been working on the upper deck of the aircraft on the way out. Only twenty-one, he hadn't been flying for long, and as they ate their dinner he confided in her about his very complicated love life. She winced at the thought of being young and single again, having to navigate the online dating scene and weed out all the weirdos that she heard were on it. Even harder it seemed for the gay men and boys like Luke who seemed to lead even more complicated lives than the girls, caught up between the noncommittal apps that promoted promiscuity and the desire to have the comforts of a relationship.

'Just like a prayer, I want to take you there…'

There it was. Her conversation with Luke stopped in its tracks as the raspy voice wailed over the speakers.

Ali, who was facing the stage at the end of the pier nearest to the entrance, spluttered as she tried not to choke on her drink, and her eyes almost popped out of her head as she registered where the awful noise was coming from. Olivia and Claire were so grateful at that moment to have their backs to the stage, as they collapsed in fits of giggles, more at Ali's facial expressions than at Julie's singing. Luke, being new, didn't have the courage to laugh in case he caused offence and just sat mute and expressionless next to them, glancing sideways occasionally to judge the reactions around him. As they turned around slowly after composing themselves they could see the glamorous and so well-spoken flight manager was writhing around on the stage doing a full Madonna routine. Olivia couldn't bear it, she had to turn back around immediately if she was not to offend Julie with her hysterical laughing. Everyone else sat frozen, mouths open, watching the performance unfold. It seemed the only person who was not dumbfounded was the captain, who was transfixed, smiling in appreciation and leaning forward eagerly anticipating her next move. Olivia cringed, perhaps something *had* happened between them last night. It wouldn't be unheard of, even though he clearly wore a wedding band.

When her performance was over Julie walked back to the table with a huge smile on her face, obviously expecting the compliments to be overwhelming. For all their laughing no one was mean and so they applauded her and told her how amazing she was.

Olivia felt a warmth towards her seeing how pleased she was with herself, it was quite sweet really and not done in an arrogant way that would have been overbearing. She was grateful, however, that the next few songs had been selected by other guests, albeit none of them were anywhere near as entertaining as Julie had been.

By the end of the evening it was safe to say everyone was a little merry and at the point that the captain suggested he and Julie do a duet Ali hastily suggested that it was probably time to go, and the others all agreed. The minibus had been waiting to take them back to the hotel and as the time difference suddenly seemed to have an effect they were all glad to be getting back to their rooms for some sleep.

The crickets were singing happily in the bushes as they walked to their rooms laughing between themselves about the night. As she looked behind her Olivia saw the captain and Julie both walking in the direction of his room and sighed. Why did so many people have to cheat on their partners? Why was it so hard to be monogamous? She knew she would never do anything again that would jeopardise her and Tom's relationship; it had been her wake up call to appreciate everything she had, and these people around her just made her want the commitment even more. Maybe it was time to speak to him about moving forward. She hadn't pushed it before but now she felt she needed the security even more. As she drifted to sleep that night she thought of how she could broach the subject with him, and in her dreams they were married and had beautiful children. Maybe it could all be hers sooner rather than later.

Chapter 15

The sound of her phone ringing woke Olivia up. It was daylight already and sunlight was streaming through the plantation shutters on her windows. She glanced at her phone, Tom on video call. Now whilst she was not vain, and whilst she knew he saw her in the mornings all the time, she couldn't bring herself to answer until she had made herself look a little more aesthetically pleasing.

Call you back in 5, she typed and took herself to the bathroom to find her hairbrush and makeup bag. She smiled as she recalled her happy dream, but decided that a transatlantic video call was probably not the best time to bring up marriage and babies, it could wait. She looked at her watch, 7am, but midday at home so she would forgive him for waking her up.

She waited for him to pick up, changing the position of the phone to give her the most flattering angle. Finally, after what seemed like an age, the connecting sign came up and Tom's face was grinning back at her.

'You're never going to guess what, babe.' She didn't think she had ever seen him so excited, he looked like he had just won the lottery.

'What?' She felt excited too but didn't know quite what for yet.

'We won the contract!!'

She thought hard. Yes, she recalled he had mentioned contracts before but had to admit she rarely payed much attention when he was talking about work, generally just nodding and making the right responses. She would have to get better at that if she was going to be a good wife!

'Which one?!' She took a gamble that he was trying for more than one, to seem like she had been listening.

'The big one with the council!'

Ah yes, she did have a recollection of him talking about this. It was something to do with all of the schools in the area, their maintenance and improvements, she seemed to recall. She knew it was a big deal and would have a huge impact on his business in a good way.

'You have no idea what this means, babe! We will need to double in size to honour it, we've started recruiting already. It's big, really big, we're made now!'

She loved that he said 'we're' – it was all for them, for their future. She wished she was at home to dance around and celebrate with him.

'Oh my god, that's brilliant, I'm so happy for you!! When did this all happen?'

He had obviously propped his phone up on his

desk as she could see him walking to the other side of his office and looking for something in the filing cabinet.

'Just this morning!' His voice was still elevated with excitement. 'We had a meeting with the chiefs at the council to tender for it, and walked away with it in the bag! I wish you'd been there, babes, we were on fire!'

Knock, knock.

Tom turned to look at the door which was out of view.

'Come in.'

'I brought champagne.'

She couldn't see her. but Olivia would have recognised that Australian accent anywhere. Her stomach was about to flip but she quickly reminded herself of her resolve yesterday to trust Tom implicitly.

Sarah walked into the picture holding a bottle of champagne and two glasses, putting them down on the desk next to Tom's phone.

Tom turned back around from the filing cabinet, still grinning from ear to ear. He looked just like a little boy right now.

'Brilliant, just the ticket!'

'It's not the best but it's all they had in the corner shop fridge.' She was leaning over, trying to open the bottle clumsily, and Olivia could see that her silk blouse was open at least two buttons lower than it needed to be.

'Hi Sarah!' Olivia put on her happiest friendliest

voice. *Keep your friends close and your enemies closer*, that old saying that her mum had often used sprung to her mind, not that Sarah was her enemy, or a threat, was she?

Sarah's face scrunched up in confusion and she looked around the room for the source of the voice. Olivia was so relieved that she had taken the time to tidy herself up a little, but still felt frumpy in her pyjamas now that she was face to face with Sarah in her tight red pencil skirt and blouse. It was a far cry from the beach babe cute look she had been sporting at the barbecue, but she must have dressed up for the meeting, she told herself. *I'm sure she won't be this provocative tomorrow,* she thought, not quite convinced though.

'It's Olivia, she's on the phone,' explained Tom, gesturing towards the desk.

Sarah took a couple of steps back and leant down to the screen, her face filling it at Olivia's end.

'Oh, hi Olivia!' She waved and smiled broadly. 'I'm just helping your boyfriend celebrate while you're away, hope you don't mind?'

'Of course not, wish I could join you!'

'We had such a result this morning, those old men in the council were so easy! What a fabulous first day for me!'

Had Sarah had a part to play in winning the contract? She didn't want to look out of the loop by asking, so was grateful when Tom offered the rest of the story.

'Yeah, I hadn't got to that bit yet, babe. Sarah

offered to come with me, she used to help with the tendering for her dad's firm so I said she could. Anyway, she had all the old farts at the council eating out of her hand and sold us ten times better than I could ever have done. She made us sound like a corporation! I couldn't have done it without her.'

Sarah had just handed him a glass of bubbly and they clinked glasses.

'Ah, it was nothing,' Sarah shrugged. 'Same deal, different continent. Dad used to take me to all his meetings like that, said it always helped to have an intelligent girl there. These men underestimate our worth, hey Olivia?!'

'Yeah.' She kept smiling but couldn't help feeling left out. She wished she was there, then she would feel differently, she was sure.

'Right. I'm off, Keira is showing me the invoicing system.' She drank the last of the champagne in her glass. 'Bye Olivia.' She waved as she walked out of the room.

'Bye Sarah, thanks for helping Tom.'

'No problem, anytime.'

She left the room and Tom turned the phone back around as he dropped into his chair, putting the champagne down in front of him.

'I didn't have the heart to tell her I hate champagne.' They laughed together and Olivia felt ok again. She didn't need to ask him any more about Sarah's input, she knew enough and it was fine. It had been her that had suggested the job after all, so she had to deal with her own jealousy or whatever it was.

They spoke about her trip and the antics of the night before and Tom watered the obligatory office plant with the champagne to make it look like he had at least had another glass; this tickled Olivia. As their conversation was coming to a natural end a message popped up on her phone.

Tennis then breakfast? It was Claire. Olivia couldn't hit the ball if she tried but would humour her friend's enthusiasm for the sport!

I'm in, she texted back.

Chapter 16

Flying back to Gatwick two days later the girls giggled in the galley about the trip. It was a safe assumption that Julie and the captain had got together. Nothing had been seen of either of them the day after the karaoke; Julie had blamed a hangover which was believable but Claire was sure she had seen them getting into a taxi outside reception the next evening, probably off for a romantic meal away from prying eyes. When they had come to the lobby for checkout though, they were acting like nothing had happened and communicated in a very business-like manner. The captain would go back to his wife now, and tell her about his dull trip, and Julie back to her home in the south of France, alone. Maybe they would engineer another flight together for a reunion, maybe they had done this before, only they knew.

Nicola was nursing a serious case of sunburn, her nose glowing like a beacon and cheeks flushed red to match the galley curtains. Being a redhead, she really wasn't made for the sun. She and Ali were highly amused as they regaled their tale of how they had been coerced by the barman into smoking a joint with him on the beach after his shift had finished, but it was Jamaica after all. Claire was relaxed and in really positive spirits, Olivia just hoped this trip would keep her friend going for a little while and that reality wouldn't bring her down too soon.

Olivia hadn't managed to talk to Tom since the video call, but he was understandably busy with the new contract to organise. She had got messages though so that was ok, and she was home for nearly a week now so would make sure they got some quality time together.

As they all said goodbye in the car park the next morning Olivia looked up at the queue of planes, visible by their landing lights, in the sky waiting to land. One after another roared over their heads, and she breathed in the smell of jet fuel that always seemed oddly comforting. Ali and Nicola were the first to leave and as Ali drove past in her Range Rover; barely able to see over the steering wheel, she stopped and lowered her window.

'Let's request another trip soon, girls!'

'Definitely,' Claire and Olivia agreed at once.

"Hong Kong!"

'Awesome idea,' agreed Claire, neither of them noticing the unsure look on Olivia's face.

With that, Ali drove off. Hopefully they would forget about it, Olivia thought, although she had a sneaking suspicion that they wouldn't. Oh well, it was highly unlikely that she would bump into Jez out there again, she was certain he didn't frequent the kind of places they were most likely to be, and even if she did that would be ok, she told herself.

She hugged Claire and watched her get in to her car, promising to see her very soon, before looking around trying to remember where on earth she had parked her own. As she was looking up and down the first officer from her flight walked towards her, heading for the bus stop looking very annoyed with himself.

'Are you ok, Jon?' she asked.

'I forgot I took the bloody train to work,' he said resignedly, trying to smile and see the funny side of his mistake. They had been away so long she guessed it was an easy enough mistake to make, presuming he had brought his car as he probably usually did, but she couldn't help laughing sympathetically at him.

'Oh dear,' she said, and waved him goodbye as he went to get the bus back to the terminal. She felt better now about not being able to find her car, which she eventually did in the very last aisle that she looked.

As she drove home she phoned Tom; she wasn't expecting him to answer, as usual, so was surprised when it picked up. Only it wasn't Tom who answered, it was Sarah, and her Australian accent cut straight through Olivia. What was she doing answering Tom's phone?

'TJ Construction, how can I help?'

'Hi Sarah, it's Olivia.' She tried to hide the annoyance in her voice.

'Oh hiii Olivia.' *Far too bloody cheerful.*

'Sorry, I meant to phone Tom, I must've called the

office by mistake.' She knew she hadn't but didn't want to come right out and ask what was going on.

'Oh no, you didn't make a mistake. I got Tom to divert his calls to here during office hours as he was missing calls from some of the clients that still use his mobile number. I can message him that you've called if you like?'

Ok, so maybe that made sense, although she wished Sarah hadn't been the one to suggest it. The last thing she wanted was for her to become indispensable to Tom, then she'd have to live with this horrible insecurity forever!

'Oh no, that's fine, I hadn't expected him to pick up anyway, you know what he's like already obviously. Good idea diverting his calls, Sarah. I'll just send him a message myself.'

'Ok, how was your flight?'

'Good thanks, always nice to be home though.' Where she was in control.

Chapter 17

Tom was still at work when she arrived home just after one o'clock that afternoon. His coffee cups from the last few days were piled up in the kitchen sink, and the remains of a takeaway were scattered across the side. She quickly tidied up and climbed the stairs wearily, thinking, as she often did on landing day, that she really must get around to employing a cleaner soon. They would have to be significantly unattractive though, she couldn't cope with leaving Tom with two beautiful women whilst she was away!

The bed was unmade as always but she didn't care, quickly showering before climbing into it and pulling the covers around her. They smelt of Tom and she breathed in deeply as she closed her eyes, imagining he was there with her. She had set her alarm for three hours' time as she wanted to surprise him after work with something special, since she hadn't been there to celebrate with him properly. She wanted to share in his excitement; after all, it was only right being that she was the most important one in his life, she told herself.

Sorry babe, not gonna b home til late, so much to do :(

Olivia sunk back down on the bed, deflated. She had just booked his favourite restaurant in town and was almost ready. She resisted the urge to be annoyed, it wasn't her style, but she couldn't help being disappointed. Perhaps if she'd checked her phone as soon as she had woken up she wouldn't have gone to any trouble but it was 7pm now, her hair was set in perfect waves and her makeup was applied with precision. She had pulled the tags off of her new Victoria's Secret underwear that she had bought in LA last month, and she had been so keen to show it to Tom. Tonight had been the perfect occasion. The restaurant was booked, and all that was left to do was choose her outfit. She shouldn't have presumed anything, but for however hard he was to get hold of when she was away, he was always home at a reasonable hour on landing day. Perhaps this new contract would change things slightly, but she would have to adjust, she guessed, as it was all for their future.

Olivia sat for a moment and collected her thoughts. How to recover the situation? Whilst she would usually have loved to slip back into her cosy pyjamas and catch up on her TV, she had gone to great lengths to look her best and was loath to waste her efforts. The solution was simple, if he couldn't come to her she would have to go to him.

She picked up her mobile and dialled the number for the restaurant.

'I'd like to order a takeaway, please.'

As she got ready to leave the house thirty minutes

later she quickly scanned the dresses in her wardrobe. A sly grin crept across her face as she reached for her long red cashmere coat… No dress needed.

The gravel crunched beneath her wheels as Olivia turned her Mercedes into Tom's yard. It was starting to get dark, and she could see light coming from the windows of the portable cabins that served as his offices. She was so focused on how she would make her entrance that she never noticed the cars parked in the shadows. Tom's was there of course but so too was a white car that she wouldn't have recognised even if she had seen it, as she had never seen Sarah's car before.

She dimmed her lights as she parked, trying to keep the element of surprise. Lifting the takeaway from the passenger seat she peered into the logoed paper bag and admired the small white boxes inside, all individually wrapped with beautiful silk bows. Cutlery, folded in white linen napkins, lay neatly on top. *Not the average takeaway*, she mused, congratulating herself.

She tiptoed as quietly and carefully as she could across the gravel in her favourite black Louboutin stilettos, and ascended the three steps to the reception office door, opening it stealthily and stepping inside. Tom's office sat behind this one, she was almost there and he hadn't heard her yet it seemed. She undid the belt of her coat, letting it drape loosely at her sides, and crept across to the door opposite.

Just as she pushed down on the handle something hit her senses, something that made her stop suddenly. An aroma of food crept up her nose and then she thought she heard two voices.

It was too late.

'Hello?'

Sarah's voice cut into her like a knife. She quickly used her free hand to pull her coat around her as the door opened and then she was face to face with her and her big, annoying, and probably fake smile. Her emotions swung from embarrassment to annoyance to wanting to knock Sarah over with the takeaway that she still held in her hand. She stood mute, unable to say a word, trying to control these feelings that threatened her composure.

'Olivia?' it was Tom. Sarah stepped backwards, still holding the door handle. Olivia looked at Tom. Firstly she needed to assess the situation; he was sat behind his desk with paper spread out in front of him. An opened pizza box sat at the end, its contents untouched, and she was grateful that she had arrived before he had eaten. Innocent looking, she thought, but of course it was, why wouldn't it be?

Tom looked at her stood there holding her coat clumsily together in the middle and suddenly realised the situation she was in. Thankfully it seemed the work that had kept them so late was not that important after all and he stood up.

'Sarah, thanks for your help, I think we've reached a good place to stop now though, it's getting late,' he said kindly. Olivia was still embarrassed, but had managed to feign a more relaxed image on the outside than she felt inside. She turned to Sarah and reiterated what Tom had said.

'Yes, thank you Sarah, we really appreciate your

hard work but I need to help Tom unwind now. It's not good for my man to work too hard.' Tom's eyes widened at the suggestive content of what Olivia had just said. She wasn't usually so forward, especially in front of people. Despite feeling slightly out of character she embraced the moment; Sarah needed to know that she was a formidable woman, and that she could never compete with her. She needed to know her place, lest she get any ideas!

Sarah look at Tom as if to disagree, and then glanced back at Olivia. She opened her mouth to say something but seemed to think better of it. She just nodded, as she walked over to where her jacket was draped on her chair in the front office.

'Goodnight then, you two, see you in the morning Tom.'

'Oh Sarah,' Olivia called after her just as she reached the reception door, 'you may as well take this pizza, I've brought Tom something much more special.' She placed her bag next to the pizza box, picking it up with one hand and holding it out towards her.

'Oh it's ok, I'm not really hungry.' Sarah waved her hand dismissively and turned back to the open door.

As she heard Sarah's car start in the car park Olivia finally let go of her coat and stood poised across the desk from Tom. He looked her up and down admiringly, and the approval in his face made her feel like a supermodel.

'Welcome home, babe. I missed you,' he said softly, raising his eyebrows slightly. The grin on his face told her he was pleased she had turned up.

'I should hope so,' she replied seductively as she let her coat slip to the floor.

Chapter 18

'It will be good for you,' pleaded Linda. If only her son would listen to her.

'I don't want to, Mum, she will make friends quickly enough. Why does it have to be *my* job? For heaven's sake, stop interfering!'

Jez retreated to the bathroom, locking the door behind him. As he looked in the mirror he rubbed his face, barely recognising the man that was looking back at him. It wasn't the same man that smiled from the happy family photos that were displayed all around the apartment, but that man was with Ness, she had been his happiness. Maybe his mother was right, maybe he did need to move on, but he just didn't know how.

He composed himself and came back to the sitting room, where Linda sat resignedly, watching the children play with their toys on the floor.

'Ok Mum, you win,' he sighed. 'When is she arriving?'

Linda beamed triumphantly. An old and dear friend had messaged to say her daughter would be coming to Hong Kong on business for a few months, and wondered if Jeremy would be able to show her around, chaperone her. Gabriella and Jez had played together when they were little but hadn't seen each other since primary school. Linda wasn't suggesting that they have a date for heaven's sake, but maybe secretly deep down she hoped there may be a spark. Unfortunately Jez knew his mum too well and had detected the hint of optimism that she couldn't hide.

'I will take her out, Mum, as friends, and that is all, ok? Don't be getting your hopes up, nothing more will come of it.' Of that he was sure, almost. A few weeks ago he would have been absolutely sure, but that night in the park, with Olivia, had stirred something inside of him. What he wasn't sure of though, and had been trying to work out since, was whether it was solely Olivia that had made him feel that way, or if he was slowly getting ready to open up to another suitable woman.

The thought though of being with someone else put his mind into turmoil. He swung between guilt over Ness, feeling that he was being disloyal to her, and overthinking how he could possibly bring anyone into the children's lives. For a moment on the night of their birthdays he had seen a glimpse of how it could be, how easily they had accepted Olivia, and how naturally she had been a part of their life for a few precious hours. She was gone now though, and he had no way of finding her, not that he had tried, but he wondered whether it was simply because she was someone special that it has seemed so easy, or if there was someone else out there that was equally as perfect for them.

Gabriella though, he mused, vaguely remembering her as a mousey kid who teased him constantly. They had nothing in common, although that was pretty typical of boys and girls, but he just couldn't imagine her as a woman, and definitely not as one that he would have any feelings other than historical friendship for. He would be a gentleman though, and take her out, show her Hong Kong as he knew it, maybe it would be nice to have a companion, perhaps a friend even. When he was honest with himself he could see that he had been reliant on his family for too long now, and that must have been hard for his mum to carry. He had shied away from his old friends, as they had been Ness's friends too, and he found their well-meant compassion and sympathy suffocating.

'Not until the end of next month. Oh, Marion will be so pleased! It will be so good for you to get out too. There is more to life than work and children, my dear son, you have a whole life to live.'

She stood up and reached high to give him a hug. He may have towered over her but he was still her little boy, and she still knew what was best for him.

'Ok, Mum.' He hugged her back, pleased that he had made her so happy.

Chapter 19

Tom was up and gone before Olivia woke up the next day. The surprise had gone down wonderfully with Tom, and they had shared a magical evening together, despite the unromantic setting of his office. Although Sarah being there had been a minor hiccup at the beginning, as she reflected on it, it had actually added to the excitement, and she had been given the opportunity to let Sarah know exactly who she was dealing with should she get any ideas about making a move on her man. After all, she didn't know that Olivia was out of character, for all she knew she was always so confident and empowered!

She was making the drive down to Southampton today to visit her sister; it was little Issy's sixth birthday and she had to have her favourite aunty there. Her mum would be there too and she was looking forward to having the family together for the day.

The two-hour drive went quickly as she talked to her friends to pass the time. She finally arrived at Shelley's small terraced house, with its pink balloons hanging over the front door, and parked behind her mum's ten-year-old Ford. She wrestled the huge teddy bear from the back seat, carrying it in front of her up the path, and pressed the doorbell.

Issy squealed in delight, first to see the bear and secondly to see Olivia.

'Aunty Livvy!!' She bounced up into Olivia's arms and buried her head in her hair. 'I missed you.' She leaned back, grinning wildly.

'Where have your teeth gone, Issy?' Olivia gasped in mock horror.

'They came out, but it's ok, the tooth fairy gave me two pounds.' She held up two fingers, so pleased with herself!

Olivia kissed her gorgeous rosy cheek and lowered her to the ground, picking up her cuddly companion again. Completely hidden by the bear, she walked into the house.

'What the hell is that?' Shelley gasped, half laughing, but trying to fathom where she would put this beast in her already overcrowded house! She did love her little sister but she was not very practical sometimes.

Olivia chuckled, putting the bear down at the bottom of the stairs and giving her sister a hug. 'Sorry sis, I couldn't resist it!' Shelley rolled her eyes, but still smiled. 'Now where's my little man?' She poked her head into the living room and looked for her nephew Luke.

'Upstairs with Oscar,' said Shelley.

'Oscar?' Olivia asked, thinking he must have a

friend over.

'His gecko.'

'Oh!'

Olivia crept up the stairs as quietly as she could, wanting to surprise the eight-year-old.

'Boo!' she shouted as she burst through the door of his small box room that barely fit his bed and toy shelves in. Luke looked up at her from his bed, beaming.

'Aunty Livvy! Look at Oscar!' He held up a small gecko the size of his hand to her. She stepped forward to have a closer look, marvelling at its beady eyes and wide grin as it stared straight back at her. She had only ever seen geckos scuttling across walls in the Caribbean and had never been able to catch one!

'Wow Luke, he's so cool, where did you get him?'

'From the reptile centre, they have the coolest animals in there, I wanted a snake but Mum wouldn't let me.' He looked disappointed.

'But Oscar looks like much more fun than a snake.' Olivia couldn't help but agree with her sister on that one as she stroked the little creature's head.

'I know.' He smiled again.

'What does he eat?'

'Crickets,' he pronounced, indicating a small plastic box on his shelf.

'Oh.' Olivia didn't know what to make of that. Whilst she was ok with bugs and spiders, seeing the swarm of crickets climbing over each other in the container did make her slightly squeamish. 'How lovely,' she said unconvincingly and Luke laughed at her.

Olivia came back downstairs and headed into the living room where her mum was sitting on the sofa. She stood up and threw her arms around her youngest daughter.

'It's so good to see you.' She squeezed Olivia tightly.

'You too, Mum.'

'How are you? How's Tom?'

'Really good, just busy with work.'

Tom rarely made the journey south with her, unless it was a really special occasion. He was always polite and friendly to them but didn't really include himself as part of the family. Hopefully that would change when they were married, but with the distance between them she doubted they would ever all be close. It didn't matter though, plenty of people didn't get on with their in-laws so she was just grateful that they did, and he never held her back from seeing them.

'Luke put Ozzy away now, time to go,' Shelley called up the stairs. They had just been waiting for Olivia to arrive before they went out to the local play centre to meet a few of Issy's friends. Shelley didn't have much money, even though her partner Mike worked long, hard hours, but they were the happiest family she knew and she loved just being with them, hanging out. It was obvious how much they all cared for each other and that they were just content with what they had. Olivia wished everyone was so easily pleased, but it was so hard not to want more when you were constantly surrounded by people making successes of their lives, and whilst she considered herself quite content, Tom was always aiming higher. Hopefully he would get high enough one day to stop climbing, and she would be able to enjoy a little more time with him.

She had to admit too that she had become quite accustomed to her nice lifestyle and wasn't sure now that she could really go back to living her old life, if she was truly honest with herself, and it dawned on her that she was wholly reliant on Tom to stay where she was. Without marriage or children, if they split up she would have nothing more than before; the house was Tom's, and whilst her job was great it didn't pay all that well. The thought unnerved her, and she brushed it away quickly. They weren't going to split up so she had nothing to worry about, did she?

As she drove home late that night her resolve to strengthen their relationship deepened. She had to find the right time soon to talk to Tom, she needed to know they were committed forever, she needed the security. She had always just imagined that one day Tom would get to where he wanted to be and then surprise her when he dropped to one knee with a small box in his hand. She never envisaged that it would be her that would push for it, nor did she have any idea how she would bring the subject up, but she would, and sooner rather than later.

Chapter 20

'I don't like the sound of her at all. Be careful, hon, you're too trusting.'

It was Claire on the phone.

Olivia leaned forward from the sofa and took her glass of red wine from the coffee table, sinking back into the oversized pillows and curling her legs up beside her. She took a sip from the glass and turned it around mindlessly, watching the dark liquid lapping against the sides. She didn't want to hear what her friend was saying but she couldn't help listening and wondering if her concerns had any depth.

'She's just young and overconfident, it's just bloody annoying that she is so bloody good at her job,' Olivia moaned.

'And that she's beautiful.'

'Yes, and that.'

'Not that you aren't though, mate.'

'Thanks!' she retorted. She had never been

unconfident in her own looks, and had always known she scrubbed up ok, but that didn't mean there weren't prettier or more attractive people out there.

'But I trust Tom, I know he only has eyes for me, that he loves me.'

'Who are you trying to convince?'

Ok, now her friend was annoying her. Why was she feeding her doubt? She needed her to talk her out of it, tell her she had nothing to worry about.

'Claire, I don't need to convince anyone, it's a fact, I know how he feels.'

'Oh hon, I know you do,' her tone changed, sensing Olivia's need for reassurance, 'and I know Tom is a good guy, I just want you to be careful. Nick was a good guy too, but he still couldn't help himself when Little Miss Sluttypants threw herself at him.'

Olivia chuckled at her friend's pet name for the girl who had stolen her last man.

'All I'm saying,' she continued, 'is that men are weak. Hopefully Tom is different, but just be careful and keep an eye on her, and if you think she is getting ideas then do something about it before it's too late.'

Olivia heard what she was saying but didn't really know how to process it. Do something? Like what? As for Tom, yes he was different, she wasn't stupid, it wasn't like she was blind to how men could be, she had kissed enough frogs before she found her prince.

'I hear you, but don't worry, I have it under control.'

Did she? It was nearly 8pm and Tom was still at work, probably with Sarah, but she hadn't dared to ask him. She couldn't turn up every night he worked late in sexy underwear, carrying a takeaway, could she? So she had had to accept it and pass the time until he got in, choosing to phone her friend rather than sitting alone letting her imagination run wild. Only this phone call wasn't really helping, it was just making her worse!

'Anyway, can we change the subject?' she pleaded, drained. 'What else is happening?'

Claire took her cue to talk about something different; she hoped her warning was enough to open Olivia's eyes to the danger, but she knew her friend well enough to know not to push things.

'Hong Kong,' she declared cheerfully.

Ugh, another subject Olivia didn't really want to talk about.

'Hong Kong?' she asked, confused, unable to relate the subject to anything other than her last flight there. She still hadn't told anyone about that, she probably never would, so she couldn't fathom why her friend was bringing it up.

'Requests have got to be in end of the week!'

'Ohhh.'

'Everyone is up for it. Nicola can't do the 11th so we were thinking either third or fourth weekend in October, what do you reckon?'

It was still only August but requests had to be submitted so far in advance they had to plan ahead if they all wanted to fly together.

'October, jeez we'll be requesting Christmas trips soon.' She was shocked at how quickly the year was going. 'I'm easy, I don't think we have any plans in October.' It was highly unlikely that Tom would take time off work anytime soon anyway.

'Fab, well let's say the 24th and I'll let the others know.'

'Great, sounds like a plan.' Olivia was sure that another two months would be enough to blur the memories of Jez enough for her to look forward to the trip with her friends. She had given him little thought in the past week or so as it was.

Just as she was saying goodbye Olivia heard the sound of Tom's keys in the front door. She put down her glass, and ran her fingers quickly through her hair, putting on her best welcome-home smile. She was ready for *the* conversation, she thought determinedly.

Chapter 21

Tom was horizontal on the sofa when Olivia came out of the kitchen with a glass for his wine. He looked tired but happy, and she squeezed herself into her usual position at the bottom of his legs.

'So how was work? I thought you were never coming home tonight,' she teased him, massaging his feet just how he liked it. He groaned in pleasure.

'Oh, babe, it's crazy. There's so much to do to set up this new contract. We need to hire more men, sort out schedules.' He stopped abruptly and looked at her apologetically. 'Anyway, I won't bore you with work stuff, how was your day yesterday?'

'Yeah, it was really good, everyone sends their love, and Issy loved her present.'

'I bet she did. Was it bigger than her?' The bear had been sat in the armchair since Olivia had bought it a few weeks back. 'I'm gonna miss the big fella watching the footie with me.'

'Yes, she loved it,' Olivia laughed, noticing that the

chair did seem rather large and empty now.

Tom had been asleep by the time she had got back from Southampton the night before, and gone again when she had woken up this morning. She would have to make sure they had some quality time together before she was back at work on Sunday; the week was going quickly and it felt like she had barely seen him.

Olivia noticed how quickly Tom had stopped talking about work and felt guilty that he thought he was boring her about it. She really should have tried harder to be more interested before now, to have paid more attention when he had told her things, but he had never seemed bothered. He had never seemed to need her to listen to him talk about himself, had always been happy just for her to talk about her trips and whatever else she had going on. It was his time now, she thought, time for her to start being more supportive, to grow up and start listening. Perhaps she would see more of him if he didn't discount her so readily from having any input into his business.

'I really do actually want to hear about work, Tom. I know I may not have always seemed interested but I like to know what is happening with you, you know, especially since it is keeping you away from me.'

She smiled and looked at him intently, focussing her mind to try and absorb any information he may want to share with her.

With that he proceeded to give her a brief summary of what had been happening at work. Olivia flinched inwardly each time he mentioned Sarah's name, although her resolve to broach the commitment subject strengthened every time she heard it. She had to admit that he lost her at points, but she didn't want to seem stupid by asking him to put things in terms she could understand too often. As hard as she tried she struggled to have anything to input to the conversation so she did her best to listen and pay attention, or at least look as if she was.

'Can I do anything to help? I'm home for the rest of the week.'

Not for a moment did she expect Tom to accept her offer, she actually expected him to laugh. What on earth could she do?

'You know, that would be amazing, babe. I think the girls could really do with a hand in the office.'

Oh! Olivia, unsure of quite how she felt or how to react, smiled as if pleased with his acceptance and took a large sip of her wine, putting the glass back down on the table. She wondered what she had just let herself in for, or if Tom knew she had no office skills whatsoever!

Tom reached up and pulled her down to cuddle him, kissing the top of her head affectionately. 'Thanks babe, I can't believe you'd do this for me. Are you sure you haven't got better things to do?'

She knew this was her chance to retract her offer, that he would forgive her flakiness as he often did.

'Nothing that is more important than helping you.' She looked up and kissed him on the lips. She felt Tom's body respond to her and decided she had said enough for this evening. She was going to help him, be his partner in work and at home, be the strong woman that was behind every man. When the time was right and she had helped him to get where he was going the next step in their relationship would be inevitable. She stood up slowly and took his hand, leading him up to the bedroom; no more talking was necessary tonight.

Chapter 22

Olivia woke to the shrill tones of Tom's alarm, and turned over as she usually did, to continue her sleep. She heard Tom go to the bathroom and was just about to drift off again when she remembered her offer from the night before. She rubbed her eyes and pushed the covers back wearily, determined not to let him down on her first day.

'Good morning,' she greeted him cheerily as she strode past him, naked, to get into the shower. She tried not to laugh at the shocked look on his face as he brushed his teeth, he had obviously not expected her to be quite so committed from day one!

She took great pleasure in choosing a knockout outfit for the office – slim Capri pants paired with a pussy bow blouse and killer heels. She would not be outdone, at least in the wardrobe department! She felt the butterflies in her stomach that reminded her that this wasn't just a fun day out, but chose to ignore them and enjoy the moment.

As they drove to work in Tom's car they both

remarked on how strange but nice it was to be in this together, or rather she had remarked and he had agreed, and as they pulled into the car park Olivia checked her face in the mirror to make sure she was the best prepared she could be.

It was a little after 8am when they arrived; nobody else was there yet and Olivia enjoyed the last few moments of her roleplay as the competent secretary. She forgot for a moment that she was actually at the office to work, remembering abruptly when she heard the sound of wheels turning into the car park. Quickly adjusting her hair in the mirror behind his door she poised herself as naturally as she could at the end of Tom's desk.

'Olivia!' exclaimed a heavily pregnant Keira as she opened Tom's office door.

Olivia jumped up and skipped across the room to hug her.

'Mind the baby,' laughed Keira.

The girls had known each other since Tom first employed Keira three years ago. Although not best friends they shared a similar sense of humour and would always have a good catch up on the phone if Olivia called the office, or sit together at the annual Christmas drinks. With the lack of other girls in the company, and there were only ten people in total as it were, they were bonded by default, despite not seeing each other very often.

'How's work?'

'Oh, same old, same old.'

'Tom says you've just been to Jamaica with your

friends, I'm sooo jealous.' Keira rubbed her swollen stomach.

'Oh, don't be jealous, you've got a baby in there, you lucky thing. You must be so excited.'

'Oh, we are, but I have to admit I'm a little scared about the birth.'

The girls looked at each other with mock horror, they both knew that childbirth was no walk in the park.

'I'll survive,' sighed Keira dramatically. 'Anyway, what the heck are you doing here at this time in the morning?'

'I've come to help.' Olivia stood up straight and smiled widely.

'Oh!'

'You don't have to sound so surprised, I have many skills other than serving people on aeroplanes you know! Perhaps I could point out the exits to people?' Olivia looked at Keira and behind her at Tom, who had been watching the two of them, and then did her best safety-demonstration arms to point out the exit, just as it opened and Sarah walked in.

Sarah looked confused but tried to smile despite herself, wondering why Olivia was pointing at her with both arms. They were obviously all sharing a joke that she had missed. Olivia and Keira tried to suppress their giggles, but failed and were unable to communicate any further without becoming hysterical.

'Forgive them, Sarah, they have clearly both been on the sherry!' called Tom from behind them. The girls looked at each other and laughed some more as Sarah walked unsurely to her desk.

'Sorry Sarah,' apologised Olivia as she composed herself, smoothing down her blouse as if that would help with her lack of control. 'It wasn't even that funny.' She looked over at Keira who was still struggling to stop laughing.

'Anyway, girls, I'm here to help. Where do you want me?' she proclaimed, and looked from Sarah to Keira eagerly.

Chapter 23

Olivia loved her first day as a receptionist, that being the role that Keira had assigned her. Being that no one, including herself, knew whether this was a one off, she had trained her in the easiest job and let her share her own desk so that she could concentrate on showing Sarah the more complicated things she needed to learn.

'Right, I'm off to grab a bite.'

Olivia looked up from filing her nails at Sarah, who was readying herself at her desk. The morning had dragged ever so slightly and she was glad to know it was lunchtime.

'I'll just see if Tom wants anything,' she said, walking towards his door.

'It's ok, Sarah, I'll take care of my man's lunch today,' Olivia said quickly, stopping her in her tracks.

Sarah looked at her, affronted. *Know your place,* thought Olivia.

As it was, Tom declined Olivia's offer of going out

for lunch; he was holed up in his office most of the day with Pete interviewing new staff, and the three girls had been treated to a steady flow of gorgeous young men, with the odd exception, waiting in their office all afternoon.

'Good afternoon, TJ Construction,' Olivia answered the phone for at least the twentieth time that day, amusing herself with the different secretary voices she could use. She had inadvertently used an Australian accent earlier, much to Keira's amusement, but thought she may have offended Sarah somewhat. Oh well, she wasn't being deliberately mean to the girl, but today was having a good effect on her own confidence and insecurities.

Suddenly a scream erupted from nowhere and the tranquillity of the office was thrown into panic.

Looking around for the source of the noise Olivia saw Sarah pinned against the wall behind her desk, still screaming and looking wildly at the floor underneath it.

The young lad who had been waiting for his interview jumped out of his seat and dashed over to her rescue, in true hero fashion, looking around the floor for the source of her horror. Sarah had stopped screaming now and was pointing at something, which he bent down and picked up, stifling a laugh.

'What the hell is happening?' Tom's door opened and he and Pete appeared, looking very concerned.

They both looked over at the lad, who opened his hand slightly to reveal a spider, and not even a very big one.

Sarah didn't seem to care that everyone was

laughing at her, she was just relieved that the beast was thrown outside, and she sank back into her chair.

'I hate critters,' she explained. 'They all want to kill your back in Oz.'

'Crikey, girl, you gave us all a fright,' said Pete, looking a little shocked by her performance. He and Tom turned and went back into their office, leaving her sat with her head in her hands trying to compose herself.

Olivia was speechless, and looked at Keira, who sat at her desk with her mouth still agape. She caught Olivia's look and rolled her eyes.

As they drove home that evening Olivia couldn't help herself from bringing up Sarah to Tom.

'Have you ever heard anyone scream that much over a spider? Silly girl.'

'I know, scared the life out of me and Pete, we thought one of you were being attacked.'

'Anyway, I'm coming in again tomorrow. Keira says she could do with me answering the phones again so she can concentrate on training Screamer, sorry I mean Sarah, up.' She chuckled at her own joke and looked to see if Tom's had found it funny too.

'No need to be mean, Olivia.' He looked at her as though he was disappointed with her cattiness and Olivia felt ashamed of herself momentarily.

'Sorry,' she said, giving him the most innocent look she could muster. He couldn't help but smile.

'That would be great if you can come in tomorrow,

babe, thanks. What's your daily rate?'

'Oh. you can't afford me, sir. I'm priceless.'

'You sure are,' he responded, and rested his hand on her knee.

Chapter 24

'Sarah, can you come in here for a moment? I need to pick your brains on something,' Tom called, leaning through the door between the offices. Sarah looked up from her computer.

'Of course.' She pushed back her chair and walked as if on a catwalk over to Tom's office, going in and closing the door behind her. Olivia looked at the closed door and tried not to let it annoy her as it always did.

It was September now and Olivia had become a regular fixture in the office, helping out on her days off. Keira was due to leave for maternity at the end of the week and Sarah was filling her shoes nicely, which irritated Olivia somewhat. She wondered what Tom needed with her now; he was always calling her in, or asking her opinion on things, and Olivia couldn't help feeling left out, and stupid, if she was honest with herself. She couldn't seem to get her head around this Australian airhead, on the outside, being so bloody competent and knowledgeable in the business. The more the new contracts bedded in the more Tom was relying on Sarah; she was pretty much his personal assistant now, and Olivia hadn't been promoted past answering the telephones. Of course Tom would reassure her that he was grateful for her help, but she still didn't understand much about how the business ran, and besides, she had a full-time job, and didn't need or want another one. Had Sarah not been Sarah no doubt she would have been quite content with her current position, if there at all.

The only thing that kept her going through their days together was she and Keira's mutual dislike for her. Of course they were astute enough not to make it too obvious, but Olivia was grateful that someone else found her annoying, although Keira obviously didn't have the added worry of her trying to steal her boyfriend.

The door opened and Tom came out. Sarah followed him and walked over to her desk, taking her jacket from the back of her seat.

'Ladies, we are just going out,' said Tom, looking over to the desk where Olivia and Keira sat. 'I've got a meeting at the council and I'm taking Sarah with me since she's met them before. We'll probably get lunch out so won't be back till this afternoon. Hold the fort for us.' The two of them headed for the door and as they walked out Sarah turned and gave them a cheerful wave.

If looks could kill Olivia would have been a murderer. She stared in disbelief as the door closed. Firstly, she fumed, Tom hadn't even acknowledged her, although she had become part of the furniture lately, she reasoned. Secondly, they were going for lunch, together, without her. And thirdly, she had freakin' waved. She may as well have held up a barrier saying 'One Up' and danced around.

'Are you ok?' Keira had noticed Olivia didn't look very happy, that being an understatement. She couldn't bring herself to answer, afraid of what she might say.

'Olivia?'

'I'm ok, or I will be in a minute.' Olivia was concentrating on taking deep breaths and calming herself down.

'It's ok, hon, it's only us two here, say what you're thinking,' coaxed Keira, aware that Olivia clearly needed to get something off of her chest, and pretty sure that it was Sarah.

'Oh Keira, is it me? Please tell me I'm being stupid, that she is just harmless and that I have nothing to worry about.' She held her head in her hands, unable to look up as she knew she wouldn't find the reassurance she needed in Keira's face.

'Oh babe, I don't know what to say.' She looked at her friend pityingly, glad that she wasn't in her situation. 'Tom's a good guy, I don't need to tell you that, but I wouldn't trust *her* as far as I could throw her.'

Olivia looked up and nodded.

'I wish to God I had never gone to that barbecue, I pretty much gave her the job and now I'm stuck with her, and feeling like this.' She put her face back down into her arms that were crossed on the desk for a moment, then looked back up at Keira. 'I don't even want to be here, answering the bloody phone all day.' She finally admitted what she had been thinking the last few weeks out loud. 'I don't think Tom even appreciates it anymore, but I feel like I need to keep an eye on her. Once you're gone I think I'm just going to quit, I'm not sure it's doing my sanity any favours being here.'

'It would be good if she just moved on, really.'

'Yes, back to the other side of the world,' Olivia agreed wearily.

'Or if she was terrible at her job and got fired.'

'If only.'

She remembered Claire's words from their telephone call a few weeks ago, they had come back to her more than once since. *Do something about it.*

Chapter 25

It was pouring with rain as Olivia drove to work the next morning, and her tears flowed down her face like the raindrops that lashed against her windscreen.

She had tried to talk to Tom about Sarah, but it had all gone so wrong and they had argued. She had first tried to belittle her, make her look stupid, but Tom wouldn't have it, defending her and stating how important she was to his business. This had upset Olivia even more, and she had accused him of fancying her. Childish, she knew, but it was funny how jealousy made you behave.

Tom had been furious. He hadn't fully seen this side of Olivia before, indeed nor had Olivia herself, and he really didn't like it. He had no time for the immaturity and neediness and had ended up sleeping in the spare room rather than talk any more about nonsense. Perhaps at one time he would have comforted her, and made her feel better, but the truth was he liked Sarah, she was indispensable to him now and he relied on her. Olivia would just have to accept her as she usually accepted everyone; he was busy and had no time for her behaving like this.

Of course Olivia hadn't had a wink of sleep, and she winced at her reflection in the rear-view mirror as she sat in the airport car park. The tears had left streaks in her foundation and her eye makeup had smudged right down to her cheeks. She reached into her cabin bag that sat in the passenger seat footwell and pulled out her makeup bag – it would need to perform miracles today.

As she stood minutes later in the bus shelter, she checked her phone, hoping there would be something from Tom. Nothing.

I'm sorry, she texted, struggling to find any more words. She thought for a moment that she should just call in sick, she had no idea how she would get through this flight. It would be easy to just call up, give her payroll number and tell them she was ill, but maybe it was best that she went away and let things calm down. She couldn't recall ever leaving on an argument before and wondered how other crew did it, as she was sure many did.

Five hours later Olivia was at 39,000 feet over the Atlantic on her way to Miami. She had sent Tom her usual message as she left and he had responded with *xxxx* – shorter than usual but it was something. The flight was busy and had taken her mind off of things for the first couple of hours, and she felt much better as she pulled the cart towards the back of the aircraft.

'Tea or coffee?' she offered the people next to her. The girl on the cart with her, Karla, was on her first flight and Olivia loved her positivity and enthusiasm.

'Any hot drinks, sir?' she beamed at the elderly man in 63C. He flashed every one of his false teeth back at her.

'Tea please, my love. Lucky me, having you beautiful ladies looking after me,' he flirted.

'Milk and sugar, or are you sweet enough?' she teased him.

He laughed and nudged his wife, making sure she had seen the attention he was getting.

'No, he's not. Give him all the sugar you've got, love,' retorted his wife, and both of the girls laughed at her quick wit. 'Forty years of marriage and he still tries to make me jealous, doesn't realise you all see him for the silly old sod that he is!'

Olivia couldn't work out if the lady was annoyed with her husband or not, or if she had resigned herself many years ago to his ways and learnt to live with it.

In her hotel room that evening Olivia drew her curtains, looking out briefly at the lights along South Beach. She couldn't face going out tonight, although some of the crew were meeting at the bar. She felt exhausted by the events of the night before, and not to mention having walked across the Atlantic. She climbed into the huge bed that was standard in all of their hotels, with its crisp, cold, white sheets, and let her head sink into the feather pillow. As she fell to sleep she thought back to the old lady on the flight and wondered if perhaps she could be like her, just accept things and learn to live with Sarah being in her and Tom's life, embrace her rather than fight her. But she just couldn't get the feeling that she couldn't trust her out of her mind, so couldn't imagine how she could ever be ok with her.

Chapter 26

It was night time in Hong Kong. Jez hung his head out as far as he could from the ferry side and watched the light show on the buildings at the edge of the harbour, feeling the fresh breeze against his face. He hadn't taken the Star Ferry since before Jacob was born and had forgotten how magical it was.

'It's beautiful.' Gabriella's voice pulled him back from his thoughts. She had linked arms with him and it felt nice to be close to someone. Coming to Hong Kong had been scary for her, but thanks to Linda and Jez she had truly enjoyed every minute of it. Thankfully the new job was exactly the same as she had done at home so the transition hadn't been at all stressful, and her time off had mostly been spent with her old companion.

As for Jez, his mum had been right. It had been good for him to meet up with her again. Long gone was the mousey kid. Gabriella, or Gabby as she preferred to be called now, had grown into a beautiful woman. She had long, highlighted, blonde hair that she wore in a fashionable cut, and she dressed in designer clothes that flattered her hourglass shape.

'Thank you so much for this, Jez. I would have been lost these last ten days without you.'

'Oh, it's been my pleasure, I needed to get back out enjoying life again.'

She looked at him sympathetically, seeing the young boy she remembered deep in his eyes. She was so sad for what he had gone through, but was happy to be a part of his moving forward.

The ferry jolted as it came in alongside the pier at Tsim Sha Tsui, and Gabby unlinked her arm as they made their way to the exit. Jez was taking her to the best restaurant in town, apparently, and she was intrigued. They made their way out of the ferry terminal and he led them along one busy road after another, eventually turning a corner into a bright market street.

'Temple Street market,' announced Jez as if introducing a show.

'Oh!' Gabby was always happy to shop but had dressed for dinner, and her heels were already killing her feet after the walk here.

Jez grinned mischievously, and took her hand, leading her through the throngs of people to the other side.

She couldn't help but laugh when he pulled out a white plastic chair from a table outside of a small café, and gestured for her to sit down. Really?!

'Don't say I don't take you to all the best places!' Jez tried to keep a straight face.

'I wish I'd made a bit more of an effort.' Gabby didn't try to hide the sarcasm in her voice, looking down at her shoes.

'Ah, sorry.' Jez hadn't given her footwear a moment's thought, he really was rusty with women and their differences! He looked at her apologetically. 'But I promise you will love the food here, Ness and I used to come all the time.' It was nice to mention Ness's name, and Gabby was always happy to listen to him talk about her. Their time together hadn't lit any fires of attraction, much to his mother's disappointment, he suspected, but they were so comfortable together, like they had been as kids, and he felt like he had a true friend in her.

'It had better be worth it,' Gabby warned him light-heartedly, punching him playfully in the arm.

After the meal, which Gabby had to admit was pretty good, she excused herself for a moment to go and buy some flat shoes she had spotted on a nearby stall. Jez leant back relaxed in his chair, listening to the noises of the market around him. He thought he detected English accents from a group of young women sat on the table behind him and so he tried hard to listen to what they were saying. Although he couldn't hear everything he did manage to hear enough to ascertain that they were flight attendants, and he found himself turning around casually to see if Olivia was with them. Of course she wasn't, he didn't even know which airline these girls worked for, and the chances of her being there right then were less than minimal.

He looked over to where Gabby stood bartering for some shoes and wondered why he hadn't had any feelings other than friendship for her, why Olivia had been different. He hoped that one day he would meet someone that he would want to be with; he had been lonely for a long time now. Perhaps one day he would see Olivia again.

Chapter 27

Olivia arrived home in the afternoon, exhausted after the long flight that had deprived her of a night's sleep. She waited up for Tom to get home from work, making sure she had prepared him his favourite meal of roast beef and all the trimmings. Usually he would be lucky if she ordered him a takeaway on landing day, so she hoped the gesture would be enough to sway his mood towards her.

Thankfully it seemed that the time away, coupled with the meal, were enough to restore the harmony, and when she went to bed early that night she felt much better about everything.

She had told him that she would come to the office the next day with him, but when she woke up to the sound of somebody beeping their horn loudly in the street he was already gone. She turned over and picked up her phone from the bedside cabinet to check the time. 10:30am, why hadn't he woken her? She remembered him asking if she was sure about coming in – wasn't she tired? – so he had obviously thought he was being nice leaving her in bed, she thought. Well it was still early, and she was going to keep her word. She got up quickly and readied herself for the day.

'Good morning Sarah,' Olivia beamed at Sarah as she walked in through the reception door. Sarah looked up surprised. Olivia hadn't been so friendly to her for a long time, in fact she was pretty sure that she and Keira didn't like her. Keira was gone now though, so maybe it was her that was influencing Olivia?

'Hi Olivia, I wasn't expecting to see you today. Tom never said you were coming in?'

'I think he thought I needed to sleep after my flight, but I thought you may need a hand?' It felt good being nice, natural, even if she was acting.

'Hell yes, I'm up to my eyes in it without Keira, and Tom needs me to sort out all these invoices.' She picked up a stack of papers from beside her keyboard. 'If you could answer the phones I can concentrate better.'

That's me, chief phone answerer, thought Olivia, irritated already.

'Of course I can, happy to help,' she beamed back at Sarah, who looked a little unsettled by the change in her. 'I'll just let Tom know I'm here.' She went to open the connecting door to his office.

'Oh, don't go in there,' called Sarah hastily. Olivia stopped in her tracks and turned around. 'He and Pete are on a conference call to someone, he told me not to disturb them,' she explained.

'Oh.' Olivia stepped back from the door and went over to the desk she had shared with Keira. 'I'll wait till he's done then.'

Almost half an hour later the door opened and Pete came out.

'Well that made my brain hurt.' He rubbed his forehead and looked at Sarah for sympathy. Pete didn't usually get too involved in the running of the business, preferring to be out there, making sure things were getting done properly. 'See you later mate,' he called back to Tom, noticing Olivia as he turned towards the door to leave.

'Oh, hi Olivia, sorry I didn't see you there,' he apologised.

'Hi Pete, is it safe to go in there now?'

'Yeah, he's off the call now.'

Olivia got up and let herself in. Tom looked surprised to see her.

'Olivia, I didn't expect you to come in today.' He looked pleased though, she thought.

'I thought you would wake me up?'

'You looked so tired I didn't have the heart.'

'Well I'm here now.' She walked over and hugged him, and he kissed her forehead as he usually did.

'That's brilliant, I really needed Sarah to help me with some stuff but had to keep her on the phones. Are you ok to cover them whilst I keep her in here for a bit?'

Olivia seethed inside. Had he just completely forgotten how she felt, or was he testing her to see if she had meant it when she said she was sorry and knew she had been silly? Or was he just a man who didn't think? 'Of course I can, happy to help.' She smiled and breezed back out of his office, hoping that she had managed to hide her feelings enough.

As she sat at her desk in the office alone Olivia struggled with her thoughts. Perhaps if they left the door open she wouldn't feel so bad. The phone hadn't rung for a while and boredom was setting in; she looked around the room for inspiration of something to do. Five minutes later she was pulling the old dusty coat stand and filing cabinet from the far corner and rearranging the furniture. As she leant down to pick up some paper that had probably been behind it for years she jumped as a huge spider ran across the floor, chasing its hiding place.

It wasn't a conscious thing, Olivia didn't think through what she was doing as she placed the glass quickly over the spider, sliding a piece of card between it and the floor and scooping it up. She moved quickly over to Sarah's desk, opening the top drawer where she kept her car keys and important things and dropped the beast into it, closing it again quickly.

She returned to her work in seconds, as if nothing had happened, and when Sarah emerged just a few minutes later she had almost forgotten that she had done anything... until she screamed!

Chapter 28

'What the hell?' Tom was furious. He had been on another call when Sarah began screaming. This time there hadn't been any interviewee hero to rescue her, and Olivia certainly wasn't going to run over to help her – she had remained firmly in her seat.

'Sarah, stop screaming!' yelled Tom, trying to make himself heard over the top of her noise.

She looked at him from where she was backed up against the wall, and for a moment Olivia felt bad when she saw the terror in her eyes. The screaming stopped as Tom walked over to the desk and followed her gestures to the cause of her actions.

Once the spider had been unceremoniously thrown out Tom walked back from the door shaking his head. 'Seriously girl, you can't scream like that every time you see a spider. Not only might I have a heart attack but if I'd been on that conference call at the time it would have been really bad.' He looked pleadingly at Sarah as he came level with her desk.

I should have timed it better, thought Olivia wryly. Just as she was telling herself not to be so mean her thoughts stopped in their tracks as Sarah practically leapt from behind her desk and threw her arms around Tom's neck.

'I'm so sorry Tom, I promise not to do it ever again.' She pulled herself back and looked at him earnestly. 'But thank you for coming to my rescue. Did you see the size of that thing?!' She smiled weakly.

Olivia coughed. Had they forgotten she was here? Had that girl seriously just hugged her boyfriend as if it was a completely natural thing to do? Had she hugged him like that before? Her mind was whirring at top speed and she wanted it to stop. 'I'm just popping out, be back in a bit.' She didn't trust herself, needed to get out for a minute, calm her thoughts down and get a grip.

Sarah looked at Olivia and took another step back from Tom, who was looking a little awkward with the situation. She hastily gathered her bag and jacket, looking at anything but the pair of them, knowing that her acting skills would not be good enough to hide her feelings from Tom if she remained in that room a moment longer.

'Anyone need anything from the shops?' she called as she opened the same door the spider had just left by, not turning around.

'No thanks,' they said at the same time, but Tom's voice sounded further away. At least he had removed himself to a safe distance, she thought, somewhat eased by this knowledge.

Olivia sat in her car in the next street talking herself down from the heights she had reached back in the office. She had to get rid of Sarah, it was so clear now. There was no way she could carry on like this, and if Sarah already thought it was ok to get that close to Tom, heaven only knew what she would think was acceptable in a few weeks or months.

If she could talk to Tom about it that would make things easier, perhaps he would put her mind at ease, but after the argument they had just had she knew this wasn't an option. So she would have to think of something, and soon, or it risked coming between them, as she couldn't possibly keep up this pretence of being ok for long.

She sat there for the next twenty minutes, as if with a devil on one shoulder and an angel on the other, both fighting to be the one to influence her. Olivia had always managed to brush the devil off before, do the right thing, but he was clinging on today. Maybe she needed him, as being nice wasn't going to help her in this situation she now realised.

'Sarah, what are you doing this weekend?'

Sarah looked at Olivia, puzzled.

'Nothing as usual.' She hadn't met the group of friends she had hoped to yet, maybe getting the job here hadn't been such a good idea as it hadn't really been a place to meet people of her own age, or gender come to that. But she was happy, and loved working for Tom, maybe a little too much.

'Me and my friend Claire are going out, would you like to join us?'

Well she hadn't expected that! Sarah hadn't been quite sure how to take Olivia lately, never knew if she was being genuine, not that she cared too much. She found boys much easier to get on with than girls, not that their girlfriends seemed to like it very much. She had a feeling that Olivia was starting to feel threatened by her too, but she was trying to hide it. It was ok, not her problem, and if Olivia felt threatened then maybe that meant she wasn't one hundred percent sure about Tom? Maybe she had got Tom wrong and he was attainable after all? Anyway, all that aside, she could do with a good night out.

'Awesome Olivia, I'd love that.'

'Saturday night it is then. We usually meet at CoCos about eight-ish. Dress to impress!' Olivia wanted this girl pretty much married off by the end of the night, and she had recruited Claire to come up for the weekend and help her. It was the nicest of all of the plans that she had gone through in the car, and she hoped she wouldn't need to move down the list too far.

Chapter 29

Surely she must like someone! Olivia and Claire were in despair. It was nearly midnight and so far their attempts to fix Sarah up with anyone had been in vain. It was as if she knew their game and wasn't going to play along. Sure, she was happy to talk to all of the boys and men who were practically queuing up to talk to her, but she would eventually wave them off.

'Nice guy but not my type really.'

'Too young.'

'Oh no, he had a small mouth.' That one had really got Olivia. A small mouth?!

'He works in a supermarket, nothing wrong with that but no thanks,' she giggled to the girls as potential beau number seven walked away looking rejected. Nothing they could say would sway the girl's opinion; she knew exactly what she wanted.

'I think it's time for another drink, girls.' She turned quickly to make her hair swing and as she walked toward the bar in her shimmering bodycon dress she made sure that she caught the attention of every man she passed.

'Argh,' cried Olivia in frustration. 'Why is she so bloody fussy? No one is good enough for her!'

'I know,' agreed Claire sympathetically, scanning the room. Maybe it was time to intervene and try to find someone suitable. 'How about over there?'

Olivia looked over to where her friend was pointing. A group of about seven or eight guys sat around a booth at the edge of the dancefloor. Their table was practically overflowing with bottles of champagne and spirits and they were all laughing and messing around, obviously already somewhat inebriated. You could tell that they had money, which obviously was high up on Sarah's list of requirements, and they were all pretty good looking too for that matter.

'I wouldn't mind one of them myself,' grinned Claire.

'We're going over here,' Claire said as she relieved Sarah of one of the three cocktails that she arrived with minutes later.

'Change of scenery,' added Olivia, struggling to make herself heard over the music.

Sarah took little persuasion to move when she realised the reason, overtaking them in her hurry to be the first at the scene. There were already groups of girls hanging around, and for a moment Olivia thought she was on a crew night out in Vegas. It was often the case in Sin City that girls would get into the big clubs for free but the men would buy tables, and then invite the girls they liked the look of most to join them for drinks. Olivia hated this there and she didn't like it any more in her own town, looking at the desperate groups that were stood around trying not to look desperate as they hoped for an invite and a free drink. Sarah, however, seemed to have no problem with any of it, nor did she seem aware of any protocol about waiting for an invite.

'Mind if I join you?' she simpered.

It seemed like five minutes later to Olivia that she was watching her friend and her enemy both throwing themselves at one of the group. She had seen Claire chat to guys before, and hook up even, she was single after all. But it seemed that a competition had evolved between the two of them for the best-looking man there and neither of them was going to back down. Olivia made small talk with the sweet little one at the edge of the booth, but made sure to mention that she had a boyfriend, and watched as Claire and Sarah now sat either side of their prey, vying for his attention.

Clearly their prey was enjoying every moment. Perhaps he hoped to be caught by them both? The drinks kept flowing and she watched as her friend seemed to be feeling the effects, her head starting to loll. She was relieved when she saw her excuse herself and the others let her out.

'Come to the toilet with me.'

Olivia linked her arm and guided her friend to the restrooms.

'That bitch,' she slurred. 'She was all over that other one until she saw I was talking to Ethan, then she had to bloody have him!'

It was true, Olivia had seen it, how Sarah had been

talking to one of the others right up until things had started looking promising between Claire and the one she now knew was called Ethan.

'You're too good for him anyway, mate.' Olivia meant it; men like Ethan weren't after a relationship. 'Let her have him, he's only after one thing.'

Claire leant against the sink. 'I know, you're right, but how dare she think she can just throw herself at him when she knew I liked him? You don't do things like that!'

'Oh, but Sarah does, I know that only too well.'

'That's it, I'm not having it, that bitch needs to learn a bit of respect and get her own man.' Olivia had rarely seen Claire angry, but she was happy to see she had a strong ally.

By the time they returned Sarah had made sure there was no room left for Claire, her competition, not that Claire had any intention of belittling herself by even trying anymore. Sarah acknowledged their return with a raise of her glass and a wink. It was as if she thought she had won something. She was obviously drunk now, and clumsily knocked the drink over as she put it down, spilling some on her conquest.

Olivia saw how he looked annoyed, and a flash of disdain crossed his face, but Sarah didn't seem to notice. It didn't stop him from putting his hands further up her thigh though and she kissed him hungrily.

'Oh, get a room,' mouthed Claire, rolling her eyes. 'C'mon, let's go.'

'Sarah, we are going,' Olivia called. She would

quite happily have said nothing but her conscience wouldn't let her leave a young girl all alone with all these men.

'Ok, bye.' She waved them off dismissively.

'Oh. just leave the cow, I think she can look after herself.' Claire pulled her friend away. Olivia went to argue. She would never leave one of her crew on their own downroute, but Sarah wasn't one of her crew, and this was Surrey, not Vegas. She looked for the one she had been talking to earlier.

'Will he make sure she gets home ok?' she asked him.

'I think they're both grown-ups, love.'

She didn't notice Claire behind her taking photos of Sarah on her phone, now that Ethan's hand had pushed her skirt up so far you could see her underwear.

Chapter 30

The bitch! Sarah looked at the picture in horror. *Why would anyone post that?*

She scrolled through Claire's post.

'Great night out – with *Olivia* and *Sarah Fischer*' it said, followed by a few selfies of the other two and then the picture that was making her head hurt even more than it had been already. She had just got up and was still feeling the effects of the night before. Two empty glasses on the coffee table in her small lounge reminded her that she had had company, not that he was anywhere to be seen now, thankfully. Well, strictly speaking she could see him, in the awful picture with his hand right up her skirt and everything on show. She quickly removed the tag and hoped that no one else had seen it, although it was past midday so that was highly doubtful.

She seethed at the thought of Claire thinking she had got one up on her when she put the picture on, she was obviously jealous that Ethan had preferred her and couldn't handle it. She wished for a moment that she hadn't invited him back though; he didn't seem to have left a number anywhere, and she doubted very much that she would hear from him again. It wasn't like her to be the one who was left, she was usually much better at reeling them in and letting them go when she was finished with them. It must have been all the alcohol, and the competition that had blurred her judgement and abilities. She was usually much better than that. Of course she would have to make it clear to Olivia that it was her who hadn't wanted to see him again. She hoped Tom wouldn't see the photo. She didn't care what the girls thought but she did care about him, she didn't want him to think she was that kind of girl.

Claire and Olivia giggled as they scrolled through the post, both still in their pyjamas on the sofa.

'I can't believe you put that on there.' Olivia bit her bottom lip, laughing nervously.

'I know, I was still drunk, I should probably take it off.' They looked at each other and both shook their heads. 'Nah,' they laughed, but it got the better of Olivia and she soon persuaded her friend to do the right thing. If Tom saw it he would think it was unkind, and that would be counterproductive.

'Yes Mum, I'm fine, stop worrying.'

Of course it was too much to hope for; her parents had seen the picture and were now worrying back home in Oz.

'Yes, he is my boyfriend!' Why did her parents still

make her feel like a little girl? A white lie about it being her boyfriend made the photo seem a tiny bit less awful she hoped.

'No, I'm not ready for you to video call him yet, it's early days. Please Mum, stop doing this,' she pleaded. 'There is nothing for you to be concerned about, I promise. I'm sure Claire didn't mean to post it, she's a friend.' Another lie, she knew that Claire had fully intended to humiliate her, and she was definitely not a friend. No girls were ever true friends.

'No, I'm not coming home, you are overreacting. I have a great job, great friends, and a normal boyfriend. I promise you I'm fine.'

Sarah hung up and sighed. She didn't think her parents would ever trust her, or stop worrying. It was their fault though, their fault for not letting her go to school and make normal friends, their fault that she had turned out the way that she had. If Mum hadn't insisted on home schooling maybe she'd have had those friends that other girls had, and have learned to consider others, not just herself.

The guys that worked for her dad had been the closest things to friends that she had when she was little, playing games with her in the yard on the days that she would go to work with him. As she had blossomed into a young woman she had noticed how they had started to look at her and treat her differently, and she liked the new kind of attention that she got. She had been amazed at how almost immediately she could make them do things for her, how they would respond to certain tones and looks that she would use. She had learnt to flirt and manipulate to get things at a young age, and loved seeing the power that she had over them. It was something she practised intently, perfecting her skills and learning new ones as she matured.

Perhaps, she had reflected as she got older, she should have considered other people more, but what young girl thinks about the man's wife, or girlfriend, or kids even? It wasn't her responsibility, she never forced any of them to be with her, and she never asked or cared if they had any other family, why would she? They weren't her problem, she didn't even know them. The guilt never came after either, when she would find out that their marriage was ruined or the jealous girlfriend would phone. Why was she the one in the wrong? She was single! She didn't even feel bad when she had to tell them that no, she didn't want to settle down with them, she knew they had lost everything but that didn't mean that she had to be their wife now for heaven's sake, they should have thought of that before. They, not him, because there had been more than one.

She didn't realise that her actions may have repercussions one day, she had been naive, and now she was here, on the other side of the world, supposedly with a clean slate and fresh start. She was trying to be good but didn't know how long it would last for.

Chapter 31

It was Monday afternoon and Olivia busied herself getting ready for her flight to Delhi that evening. It was another flight known to be demanding but hopefully they would be tired and not want too much from her, she thought doubtfully. She packed her black shift dress and heels, that would do for the restaurant, and some casual clothes for the trip to the hotel spa. Massage and eyebrow threading, that would be her treat this trip, she thought, and maybe a facial. The exchange rate with the rupee was so good a girl could really spoil herself there.

She teased her hair into place around her foam hair doughnut, the easiest of all her flight hairstyles, pinning the loose ends in around the edges and fixing it all with some spray. There, the perfect work hair. She leaned in closer to the mirror and applied a slick of red lipstick to finish off the look, standing back and admiring the perfectly groomed flight attendant that was looking back at her from the mirror. Putting her makeup into her cabin bag she mentally checked that she had everything that she needed. Passport, ID, cabin shoes, torch, check.

She rummaged quickly in the kitchen on her way out, looking for snacks to take with her. In the fridge she noticed some gammon that would need using up whilst she was away. She glanced at her watch to see if she would have time to pop by the yard, pleased when she saw that she would, and took it out. Tom would be sure to appreciate her taking him some late lunch on her way to work and she worked hastily to make a sandwich fit for a king, leaving the house carrying his lunch in a bag moments later. She wanted to check that Sarah had got home safely Saturday anyway, as she couldn't help worrying despite her dislike for the girl. She also needed to check that Ethan had worked out as planned and that she could go away and enjoy this trip without the extra worry baggage that she had taken with her lately. She hoped that Sarah was as persuasive as she thought she was, as men like Ethan were hard to keep interested, and she was glad that Sarah had stepped in before Claire had been sucked in by another man who wasn't real.

As she parked next to Tom's car she changed back into her work heels; there was no way she was walking in there wearing the slippers that she wore for the drive to and from the airport. She checked herself in the mirror before walking as glamorously as she could, in case anyone was watching, across the gravel to the door.

No one was in the front office, although she had definitely seen Sarah's car outside, but despite wanting to burst into the back office she knocked first, just in case they were in a meeting.

'Oh, hi Olivia.' Sarah couldn't manage to fake pleasure at seeing her as she opened the door, but smiled nonetheless.

'Hi Sarah.' Olivia, however, was more than happy to see Sarah, especially in front of Tom. 'So glad to see you got home ok, I've been worried about you, I hate leaving people behind.' She could see Tom was watching. She had told him already about Ethan, and how they had tried to get her to come home with them but she wouldn't, but she needed him to see that she really was concerned about Sarah, that she was the better person.

'Oh no worries, yeah I think I definitely had a bit too much to drink so I just took myself home.'

'So how about Ethan?' Olivia winked at Sarah, teasing, waiting for her reply.

'Who?' She looked puzzled, as if trying to remember something she may have forgotten.

'Ethan, the guy you hooked up with?'

'I didn't hook up with anyone, Olivia, I came home on my own. I couldn't find you guys so I just got in a cab, presumed you were still in there trying to find a man for Claire?'

Olivia reeled inside. The lying little minx. How could she just stand there with that fake smile on her face and make out she was perfect, whilst making her and her friend look like the desperate ones who were hunting for men?! There were photos to prove it, if only she had let Claire leave them on there, or shown Tom first. Why had she made her take them down? Worse still, she had made out that they had just left her there, and Tom was looking at her as if she had made it all up.

Olivia didn't know what else to say. She was no match for Sarah, she had never come up against anyone like her before so she didn't have the artillery to fight back.

'Oh, I must've got it wrong, sorry, obviously we all had one cocktail too many. Anyway, I thought I'd just pop in and say goodbye on my way to work.' She walked over to give Tom a kiss and could feel Sarah's eyes following her. 'I brought you some lunch.' She put the bag on the table.

'Oh, thanks babe.' Tom got up and hugged Olivia, kissing her quickly back. Sarah didn't make any moves to leave the room, and Olivia was still so unsettled by what had just happened she didn't have the focus to ask her to.

'Sorry, we were just in the middle of something important so I can't leave it right now, have a good flight though.' He looked at her earnestly, holding her by the shoulders.

'Thanks, I will,' she lied. This was becoming a habit now, leaving with this horrible feeling in her stomach. 'I'll let you get back to it, see you Wednesday. Love you.' She didn't care if Sarah was there, she did love him, and she kissed him again.

Sarah stood by the door still holding the handle, and closed it behind Olivia almost triumphantly, it felt. Olivia raged, not knowing what to do as she stood on the other side of the closed door. She looked at Sarah's desk for inspiration and saw the pile of invoices stacked up ready to be sent out, next to her monitor. She thumbed through them, taking out random ones, walking over and putting them in the paid file of the filing cabinet. She didn't know much about the business but she had done enough filing there to know where these things went. Obviously her first plan had failed miserably and she would need to up her game. Sarah needed to become less indispensable.

Olivia spoke firmly to herself on the drive to work. She had to stay calm, and she had to be clever. Getting herself worked up every time Sarah worried or annoyed her was hurting no one but herself. She had a job to do tonight and she was not going to endure another flight like before where she took her problems with her. She would leave them behind for now; nothing was going to happen in two days away and she was going to enjoy herself as she had planned to, then she would have something positive to tell Tom about when she got back.

Chapter 32

The self-counselling helped, and she felt almost uplifted by her decision to leave her worries at home. It didn't matter how many passengers demanded tea whilst shaking their head at her, or how many times she had to put her gloves on to clean the toilets, she enjoyed the flight out. It was very much a case of cultural awareness on this route, and she laughed as the newer crew came into the galley time after time saying all of the things she had said herself when she did her first few Indian flights.

'No please, no thank you just…' Jamie bobbed his head from side to side mimicking the passenger who had just stopped him and asked for tea. 'And those toilets are disgusting.'

Olivia laughed out loud and Avanash, one of the Indian crew members, pretended to look affronted.

'Are you making fun of my culture?' he said, with the same head movements.

Jamie looked embarrassed for a moment before

Avanash and Olivia collapsed in fits of giggles.

'Try not to take it personally, Jamie,' Olivia said kindly. 'It's not personal, it's just cultural, they don't know you are expecting them to have the same manners as us.' This was mainly true of the older customers who weren't accustomed to the western ways as much. As for the toilets, this way was bad enough but the flight home carrying all those people with Delhi Belly would be much, much worse, she thought to herself, but she would let him find that out then.

The meal service filled the cabin with aromas of curry and despite no one wanting to go to sleep as she had hoped they would it was easy enough, perhaps because the crew were all such hard workers, and they laughed a lot. They even laughed as they laid cardboard boxes and blankets on the back galley floor for their rest. Sleep was sleep, even if you had to spoon with practical strangers on the floor like homeless people, because the stupid aircraft you were on had no crew rest area. Officially they were meant to take their breaks sat upright in their jumpseats in the galley on full flights, but that was torture, they didn't even recline.

'Right, keep guard, see you in an hour.' Olivia pulled the curtain across, leaving two of the crew posted outside to intercept any passengers, or heaven forbid, the flight manager.

'We will, sleep well,' came the reply, and she did, despite the conditions!

It was morning in Delhi when they arrived and Olivia had slept so well on her break she didn't feel the need to go to bed. The layover was so short that she just wanted to make the most of it; this hotel was one of the best that they stayed in. It seemed that the poorer the country the more luxurious the hotel they were put up in, and The Grand was exceptional. Her room was huge, and the bathroom hosted a jacuzzi bath *and* a wet room. Olivia soon put the upmarket complimentary toiletries that she would not use into her wash bag ready to go into the guest bathroom at home. She showered and made her way down in the lift to the vast marbled reception area, with panoramic views out over the pool through the glass back wall. She walked carefully down the polished steps at the back and along the corridor, passing the small shops selling pashminas and jewellery, resisting the moustached local salesmen in their pressed white shirts who tried to stop her, and made her way to the salon at the end.

Jamie was there in a seat when she arrived, waiting for a massage.

'I'm only here for the happy ending,' he joked, and Olivia looked quickly around her to see if anyone had heard. It was rumour that the male masseuses would give the boys a 'happy ending' to their massage if they paid a little extra, and Olivia dreaded to think whether it was true or not. She never failed to be shocked by people's things that she heard in her job, even after all these years.

'Oh, well I hope you get what you want.' What else could she say?

A small Indian girl came out of the salon and stepped behind the desk.

'How can I help you, madam?'

Olivia woke up to the girl calling her softly.

'Madam, you are finished.'

'Oh, thank you.' Olivia pushed herself up slowly from the massage table and sat for a moment rubbing her eyes. 'Sorry, I think I fell asleep.'

'No problem, madam.' The girl smiled. Pretty much every crew member that came in here after their flight did the same.

She paid for her treatments and left the salon feeling more relaxed than she had done for a long time. A few hours by the pool would pass the time until dinner, she thought, and she quickly went back to her room to get her bikini on.

The weather at home was turning autumnal and it was nice to feel the sun on her skin once again. She turned the pages of the magazine she had brought from the plane, lazily looking at the lives of people she didn't know, and scrutinising them. Several of the other crew lay on the beds alongside hers, and she caught snippets of their conversations that made her feel better about her own problems. She could have brought it up, seen what opinions the girls had about Sarah, but she didn't want to think about it now, she wanted to stay in her happy, relaxed bubble a little longer.

'Right, I'm going up to get ready.' Olivia looked up at Sophie who had stood up and was putting her beautiful green kaftan on over the top of her swimsuit. 'See you girls in reception at seven.'

They howled with laughter as the three yellow and green tuk-tuks carrying the crew raced along the highway. Thankfully there was little traffic as it was now eight o'clock, although with a four-and-a-half-hour time difference Olivia was never quite one hundred percent sure of the time here. The trick was to turn your watch upside down but then the hands never seemed to be on one hour or another so you still had to guess a little. Back home everyone was at work or driving their sensible cars around but in another brief moment of 'I love my life' she appreciated everything. The streets were dark and she watched as they passed a world that was so different to hers at home. Carefree and without a thought to seatbelts and safety they whizzed past, whole families piled onto scooters and cows roaming across the street. Stalls selling their wares were lit up along the sides of the street and people gathered around them after a long day at work. Some would go back to the new apartments that housed those that had found success in New Delhi, others would return to their makeshift shelter with their families, here from the countryside to find work. Such was life here; some had it all and some had nothing.

A swarm of children surrounded them as they pulled up at the restaurant, hands stretched out begging for money. Their white teeth contrasted with their dirty faces as they smiled and chattered away in their mother tongue. It was so hard to know what to do for the best. The government said not to encourage begging, and they knew that the money would go straight back to the man hiding in the shadows, but what harm could a few pounds do? It was worth so much more here. Thankfully one of the crew had prepared for it and pulled out pens and notepads from her bag. They grabbed eagerly at the gifts and ran off happily to try out their new toys.

'Good thinking,' the other crew congratulated her, all making a mental note to bring similar things next time, although most would forget despite their good intentions.

The restaurant was dimly lit, with wooden floors and candles flickering in lanterns on long wooden tables. The captain had reserved a table here at The Copper Chimney for ten and the Indian waiter led them up the stairs to their seats, coming back immediately with local beers and bottled water.

'Anyone for antibac?' Kim, the flight manager asked. She passed a small bottle of antibacterial gel along the table, as it was more often the bacteria from things that they touched that would upset the stomach here than the food. Olivia squirted a generous portion in her hand and passed the bottle to Sophie, rubbing her hands together vigorously.

She handed her phone to the waiter when he came to take her order and smiled as he took a photo of them all enjoying themselves. She would post the pictures from here as soon as she got back to her room; she felt like she needed to move the ones from Saturday night into the archives and move on. She hated that her life had been hijacked, she wanted to go back to this, the happy life she had before, the good trips and happy home life. If she wanted it then she needed to make it happen, no more hoping or trying to be nice.

Chapter 33

She couldn't have hoped for a better result. Olivia sat at her desk the following week pretending not to notice the drama that was unfolding between the bookkeeper, who was in on his fortnightly visit, and Sarah.

'I have no idea why, Adam. You must have added it up wrong, don't look at me.'

Olivia could see Adam's neck flushing red around his collar and the normally quiet and placid man was looking at Sarah with wide eyes.

'Right, I'm going to have to get Tom out here, this needs sorting out.' His voice was tight, as if trying to hold in what he really wanted to say. Sarah barely looked up; she knew she hadn't done anything wrong, and geek-type men like Adam couldn't ruffle her feathers.

Adam disappeared into Tom's office carrying the books under his arm, closing the door behind him.

'What's all that about?' Olivia asked innocently.

'Damned if I know, guy can't add up I reckon. I'm sure it's something simple but he needs to calm down. Last thing Tom needs though, he's stressed already.'

'Sarah, can you come in here please?' Tom's shout startled both of the girls, and Sarah looked sharply at Olivia, pushing her seat back quickly.

It seemed like they had been in there ages. Olivia wished she could be a fly on the wall, imagining the moment when they worked out that Sarah's incompetent filing had caused all the trouble. She wanted to save them the time of trying to work out where the discrepancies laid but obviously couldn't if she didn't want to be found out.

Tom emerged some time later and stomped loudly across to the filing cabinet, opening the same drawer that Olivia had done last week and extracting several files, slamming it shut again. He looked at her as he walked back, lips pursed, rolling his eyes upwards.

'Can I do anything to help?' She at least had to offer.

His face softened slightly and he shook his head before disappearing back into the room.

Another hour passed slowly before the door opened again. Sarah came out first and she seemed different from the person she had been when she went in there. Her posture, normally so perfect, was now slouched, and a furrow had formed between her eyes. She looked confused, and Olivia could almost read her thoughts, trying to work out how she could make such a big mistake.

Adam came out shortly after, and turned at the door to shake Tom's hand.

'Right, glad we got to the bottom of that, see you in two weeks.'

'See you then,' replied Tom as he walked towards Sarah's desk, putting a pile of files next to her. 'Can you please put these away, in the right place this time?' He sounded exasperated, and disappeared again quickly to resume the work he had been doing before all of the drama.

'I know I wouldn't have done it, sure I wouldn't have.' Sarah looked at Olivia for reassurance.

'We all make mistakes, hon, don't be so hard on yourself.'

'But I've never done anything like that before.' She held her head in her hands.

Olivia could see her trying to work out what had happened and hoped she wouldn't remember the details of the day that those invoices had been on her desk before.

'Why don't you get out of here for a bit? Go and get some fresh air.'

Sarah looked at her gratefully. 'Yeah, that's a good idea, thanks.'

No sooner had she left Tom came out holding his jacket and car keys.

'Where's Sarah?' he asked, noticing the empty desk and the files still where he had left them.

'I told her to go and get some fresh air, the poor girl was so upset.'

'Well hopefully she won't be long, she needs to sort out the mess she made.'

'Ah, don't be too hard on her, Tom.' Olivia wondered if she was being too nice now. 'She won't be long.'

'Easy for you to say, she hasn't just caused you a bucketload of trouble.' He smiled and his shoulders relaxed somewhat. 'Anyway, now thanks to her I'm over an hour late, I should've been at the Ludlow site ages ago.' He bent down and kissed her before heading out. 'I don't suppose I'll be back before late now so tell Sarah to lock up. See you at home.'

'I'll make us something nice for dinner,' she called after him.

It must have been because she was thinking of Sarah that Olivia slipped into her Australian accent as she answered the phone. She was getting quite good at it now with all the impressions she had done of her to Claire lately.

'Of course, I'll get him to call you first thing in the morning when he's back in the office.' She hung up and wrote down the name of the man from the council that needed to speak to Tom as soon as possible. He could wait until tomorrow as long as it was first thing, she mustn't forget to tell him. Although, she thought, it wouldn't strictly be her that forgot would it, it would be Sarah. She screwed up the memo and threw it into the bin.

Chapter 34

Sarah closed the door of her apartment behind her and walked solemnly along the hallway to the living room. She dropped her handbag onto the floor as she sat heavily on the sofa and put her face in her hands, staring at the grey carpet through her opened fingers. Life had been so calm and good up until recently but she could feel things unravelling and worried that the good times may be coming to an end as they always seemed to.

She had sworn blind that she hadn't taken the phone call, of course she would have passed the message straight on, she always wrote things down. The man who had phoned though, urgently needing to speak to Tom, had been quite sure that he had spoken to an Australian girl and she was the only one around.

There were the misplaced invoices too. She knew she hadn't done it, she was too organised, too good at her job. Why would she have put them in the paid file before she had even sent them out? She thought hard, going over everything that had happened since she had printed them up, but it was well over a week ago now and she just couldn't find the answer.

Sarah knew that she wasn't perfect, and sometimes she might make a small mistake, but never any this big, and never this many. She could tell Tom didn't believe her though, that he thought she was incompetent, and she worried that he might be starting to think she wasn't the right person for the job anymore.

She clutched at her hair with clenched fists. Was she going mad? There must be an explanation. What tied the two things together? She knew she hadn't done either, so who had?

Of course! It was like Big Ben was striking the hour in her head as she realised the connection. Olivia! Olivia had been there last Monday when she was sorting the invoices, and she had been here 'helping' again yesterday, the day of the phone call. She must have answered the call in that phoney Australian accent she had heard her use once when Keira was here, and either deliberately or not, forgotten to pass the message on. But the invoices, she wasn't working that day, so she would have had no reason to file them. She must have seen them on the desk when she dropped in on her way to work. So it *had* all been deliberate.

Sarah felt her senses wake up. She knew Claire had tried to make her look bad, but now it seemed Olivia had too. Why, oh why did she have to do that? She had tried so hard to be good. Olivia had been so kind to her in the beginning that she had resisted all of her urges to pursue Tom, despite her feelings for him.

Now though, she had made it personal. She wasn't a friend anymore, and she had suspected that for a while, so she no longer had to consider her feelings as her counsellor had told her she must.

'You want to play like that, you'd better be prepared for the consequences,' she whispered. If Olivia had really tried to frame her then there would be a price to pay. She wouldn't get away with it.

'Maybe just give her one last chance.' Olivia couldn't believe she was saying it, it certainly wasn't what she really meant.

'I don't know babe, I don't have time to keep cleaning up after her. I don't think you understand how hard I had to work to get back on side with him, he was furious that I hadn't called back. I need to be reliable or they can just cut the contract.'

'I'm sure she won't make any more mistakes, she will be really upset with herself about this.' Argh, why couldn't she just twist the knife in and be done with it, feed his doubt and get Sarah out once and for all? She could sense that he might just be speaking in the heat of the moment though, that he didn't really want to get rid of her yet, and if she was too pushy she might end up being the one who looked bad in the end. She would feel stupid if she encouraged him to get rid of her and he didn't.

'You're right, as usual.' He extended his arm around her shoulder and pulled her towards him on the sofa. 'One last chance.'

As Olivia leant against Tom's chest, thinking of ideas for Sarah's one last chance the buzzer from the electric gates sounded in the hallway. She looked at her watch as she sat up – 8:15pm, who on earth was turning up unannounced at this time?

'I'll go.' Tom pushed himself up from the sofa and left Olivia where she was. She couldn't hear who was speaking on the intercom but was intrigued when she heard him press the buzzer that opened the gates, and open the front door moments later. As she heard his footsteps coming back along the corridor she could hear another voice, female, and just as her stomach flipped as she realised who it was, Tom walked back into the room followed by Sarah.

Tom was holding a bottle of whisky and Sarah walked over to Olivia with a beautiful bunch of flowers wrapped in tissue paper, handing them to her.

'I just wanted to apologise for my mistakes lately. I couldn't wait until Monday, so I just needed to come over and tell you both in person.'

'Sarah, you didn't need to do this.' Tom studied the label of the bottle, obviously impressed with her choice and glad that she had bothered nonetheless.

Olivia stood up with her flowers. 'I don't deserve these, you really shouldn't have.' She wondered what Sarah was playing at.

'No Olivia, you were so nice to me the other day when I had filed the invoices wrong, and I appreciate it.' She turned to Tom. 'Tom, I am so sorry for all the extra stress I have caused you this week, I know it was the last thing you needed. I had a lot on my mind, not that it is an excuse, but I promise you I won't make any more mistakes.'

'Oh don't worry, no one died.' Tom had been won

over and forgotten his words of just ten minutes ago, it seemed. Olivia walked towards the kitchen to find a vase, trying to hide her annoyance that Sarah was in her home.

'Phew, I thought I might have got the sack on Monday,' Sarah laughed. 'Lovely house by the way,' she said, looking around her admiringly.

In the kitchen Olivia couldn't hear them anymore. She fought her urge to throw the flowers in the bin despite them being truly exquisite. She looked in the cupboard for something to put them in, taking out the ugliest vase that she could find, one she had inherited from an old aunt with gaudy flowers painted on cracked porcelain. She returned to the living room a few moments later, ready to thank her, and show her out promptly, but no one was there. *Tom must be showing her out already,* she thought, looking around the room and wondering where she should put the flowers so that she wouldn't have to see them too often. Placing them on the windowsill, she drew the curtains in front of them; tomorrow she would think of somewhere better.

Chapter 35

A few minutes passed and Tom still hadn't returned. Olivia checked the front door, but it was shut, and when she opened it she saw Sarah's car was still in the driveway. Her heart raced for a moment as she wondered where she had gone but as she walked back into the house she could hear music coming from downstairs in the den and realised exactly where they both were. It really was time for her to leave now, she thought determinedly.

They obviously hadn't heard her coming down the stairs; admittedly she had trodden very lightly. From the doorway she watched them sat with their backs to her at the black leather-trimmed bar on the far side of the room, both leaning forward and obviously in deep conversation. Sarah's body language sat uncomfortably with Olivia, her legs crossed and facing toward Tom, with little room in between the pair, and she was flicking her hair back whilst laughing at a joke to which she was not privy. To a passer-by in the street glancing in a bar window somewhere, they could have been a couple who had just met and were getting to know each other, with all the signals of chemistry between them.

'There you are.' Olivia put on her biggest fake smile, but couldn't help raising her eyebrows as she looked at Tom when he turned around.

'Sorry babe, I was just giving Sarah a tour of the house and we ended up here.' He raised his glass guiltily, gesturing to the bottle that Sarah had just given him sitting open between them. Sarah turned slowly on her leather stool, and Olivia saw she too was holding a glass. *Of course* she liked whisky, she seethed inwardly. She was the only woman she knew who did, and she guessed that they had been bonding over their mutual love of the stuff.

'Amazing house, Olivia, I love it down here!' she gushed.

'Thanks.' Olivia's mind whirred as she thought of how to get this girl out of her house ASAP. 'It's great when we have our friends over.' *And you aren't one of them*, she thought. She walked across the tiled floor that acted as a dancefloor, glancing at the retro jukebox on the left wall that was playing loudly.

'Join us, Olivia. Have a drink,' Tom urged.

There were many reasons why Olivia did not want to join *them*. Firstly, that would quite possibly extend Sarah's stay in her home, and involve her having to act like she didn't mind. Also there was the matter of her 5am start tomorrow and a flight to New York. Tom knew she had work in the morning, and that she needed an early night. She seethed.

'I'd love to but you know I have work in the

morning, babe, and so have you.' Tom had already said earlier that he needed to go to bed early as he had to go in tomorrow too.

'Oh, a couple won't hurt. It would be a shame not to do this bottle justice. Have you any idea how special this whiskey is?'

'No, Tom, I don't,' she answered curtly. She couldn't hide it any more. The awful screeching music that she could only presume Sarah had selected was giving her a headache and she really wanted her to leave *right now*. Her irritation was clearly lost on Tom though, it obviously hadn't occurred to him that Olivia, who always loved to entertain, wouldn't want to do so tonight.

'Oh, one won't hurt.' He got up and went behind the bar, taking a glass from underneath and dispensing a shot of rum from the optic behind him into it. He reached into the small freezer that sat neatly at the back and took out some ice, putting it in the glass and handing it to Olivia with a can of Coke.

'Just one then. No offence, Sarah, but I have to be up early.'

'Oh, no offence taken Olivia, don't mind me if you want to go to bed,' she replied as if butter wouldn't melt.

Was she stupid? Did she think she would leave her alone down here with Tom while she went up to bed? She looked at Tom to see if she had an ally but he was busy putting more ice and whisky into their glasses; he obviously had the taste for it now and wasn't throwing Sarah out anytime soon.

'Do you think you should have any more when

you are driving, Sarah?'

'Oh, one more won't hurt, I can handle my whisky.' She picked up her glass and raised it to Olivia. 'Cheers.'

'Stop being so boring, Olivia, it's not even nine o'clock.' Tom looked at her and she felt her face flush red.

Olivia sipped her drink, welcoming the effect of the alcohol which seemed to reduce her heart rate. She tried her best to join in their banter about work but had to admit defeat as Tom poured their third whiskey, larger than either of the last two.

'I have to go to bed. Tom, will see you out Sarah?' *Hopefully very soon*, she thought.

As she laid in the bed sleep was evasive. She wondered what they were talking about in the den, and how much closer to Tom Sarah had moved her chair. Eventually she heard their voices in the hall and she tiptoed to the front bedroom to watch Sarah leave. As the front door shut and she watched her get into her car she took her phone from her dressing gown pocket. She strained to see the registration number of her car as it drew through the gates and dialled a number she had never needed to use before.

'Hello, emergency services, which service would you like?'

'Um, the police please,' she said quietly.

A short silence followed before she heard her call connecting.

'Hello, police.'

'Hi, I'd like to report someone who is currently driving their car after having too much to drink.'

She hadn't heard Tom come up the stairs, and she jumped when she felt his hand on her shoulder. She hung up the call immediately, wondering how much he had heard, but when she turned around she could see by his face that he had heard enough.

Chapter 36

Tom just couldn't believe what she had done, not that she had got as far as giving Sarah's details to the police, but the fact that she had even contemplated it had been enough. They hadn't really rowed, perhaps that would have been easier, but the look of disappointment on his face had been enough to crush her. 'I don't know who you are anymore.' Those were his words, and she couldn't get them out of her head. Again, she had contemplated calling in sick for her flight but she knew he would need time to calm down, and she probably needed to go away and get some sleep to stop her getting too emotional. It was just a bullet to New York with a minimum layover, she would be too busy to think too much, she reasoned, and when she got back on Sunday she would make it up to him, again.

'Catered full, my love. Fifty-three kosher meals, I'm afraid.' The caterer looked at Olivia apologetically.

Oh my word, she thought. Today was going to be

a hard day! Whilst she didn't mind a few special meals, having to hand out fifty-three kosher meals by hand before they could even start the meal service was not ideal.

'Ok, thanks, not,' she joked.

'Sorry,' he laughed and handed her paperwork to say she had seen all of the catering. She scribbled her initials and gave it back.

'Have a good flight.'

'I'll try,' she sighed loudly, and watched him walk up towards the front of the plane to check the other galleys. She looked around at the vastness of the Boeing 747, with its four hundred economy seats, their galley today being situated in between the four doors as they were known, or the fourth set of doors down from the front. With five sets of doors in total, and a sixth on the upper deck, it was worthy of its iconic status as the Jumbo Jet, and it held a *lot* of passengers! She was happy to be kept busy today though.

It was like when you go on a long drive and suddenly realise you can't remember any of the last twenty miles, she thought, as she found herself putting away the last meal cart without being able to recall much about giving the meals out. She pushed down the brake and pulled the red latch down over it, checking over the other carts to make sure they were all secure in their stowages. The crew began to filter in, looking through the ovens for food now that they had a chance to eat, and Olivia stepped out into the aisle to make some room.

Now that things would be quiet for a while she

decided to take the opportunity to go and see the pilots, and she made her way to the stairwell that led to the upper deck.

'How's it going up here?' she asked the girl in the upper deck galley at the top of the stairs. Olivia didn't even remember seeing the pretty, petite blonde girl in the briefing, let alone know her name.

'Not bad,' she replied cheerfully, clearly free from the worries and anxieties that Olivia had brought with her today.

'I'm going up to see the boys, do you want me to take anything?'

'No thanks, Adrian just took them in a cup of tea.'

Olivia had to think for a moment before remembering that Adrian was today's manager of course. She really wasn't at her best.

She smiled and walked swiftly to the door right at the front, tapping the access code into the keypad and looking up at the camera above her.

Click. The door unlocked and Olivia entered the flight deck, closing it quickly behind her. She had heard about the days before terrorists started flying planes into buildings, when the flight deck door wasn't locked, and children would queue up outside to meet the captain on some routes. It was a shame that now they had to stay locked in this small cockpit pretty much all flight and so she always made an effort to go and see them if she got a chance.

Adrian was already in there and she leant against the jumpseat he was occupying on the right of the door behind the two pilots. Olivia tutted as her hair caught in one of the hundreds of buttons that lined the ceiling, and released herself carefully lest she should pull something important. She recognised both of the pilots but didn't know them well so they talked through the list of questions that were standard.

'Any plans for New York?'

'Did you have to travel far this morning?'

'What's your next flight?'

The list wasn't exhaustive; when you met so many different crew it was useful to have the small talk ready.

'How are things going down the back?' Adrian asked, looking up at Olivia.

'Yeah fine, once all the specials were done!'

'Shall we sort some breaks out then?'

They both looked at their watches to ascertain whether there would be enough time between now and the last service to make it worthwhile.

'We could probably manage an hour if we split the crew in two?' Olivia calculated, allowing two hours at the end.

'Let's do it, I could do with a power nap myself. I'll be back later guys,' he said to the flight crew, and they both signalled their goodbyes, turning back to the controls. Olivia checked through the spy hole to make sure that no one was outside the door before opening it, and led the way back out into the cabin. Just as they got to the stairs the plane jerked and suddenly Olivia felt herself lift off of the floor as they hit an area of clear air turbulence. She reached out to grab the handrail but slipped and lost her footing, tumbling forward down the steps. She clutched at the rails to stop her fall, and felt a crack as her left arm twisted backwards, sending excruciating pain that made her cry out. The seatbelt signs pinged on.

'Cabin crew, take your seats,' came the captain's voice over the PA.

'Oh my god, are you ok Olivia?' called Adrian from the top of the stairs. He was on his knees holding onto the handrail with one hand and reaching out to her with the other. She tried to turn herself around without moving the hurt arm too much, and let Adrian help her up and onto the jumpseat at the top of the stairs. She sobbed with the pain and held her injured arm against her body to immobilise it.

'Are you ok?' asked the girl from the galley as she made her way past in the direction of the jumpseat at the upper deck doors, holding on tightly to the seats she passed. Olivia nodded, bravely biting her bottom lip.

Adrian put his arm around her shoulders to comfort her, unable to do much else as the plane struggled to find a smoother path. They could hear cries from downstairs and he took the phone from next to their seat to make an announcement.

'Ladies and gentlemen, it does appear that we have encountered an area of clear air turbulence. This is an unfortunate situation but please rest assured that it is nothing to worry about and the captain is currently navigating us out of it. For now, please make sure your seat belts are fastened and the crew will be with you should you need any assistance as soon as it is safe to do so.'

He put the phone back in its stowage and looked at Olivia, glancing down at her arm with a concerned look on his face.

'It must be awful down the back.' Olivia tried to take her mind off of the searing pain. It was true that turbulence was always significantly worse as you neared the thinner tail end, and she hoped that no one else had been hurt.

Chapter 37

Olivia saw the flashing lights of the emergency services waiting on the ramp as they taxied onto stand. She had been right about down the back, they had felt the full force of the turbulence, with stories of people coming inches off of the ground. One unfortunate man had landed so heavily in the confines of the toilet that he had hurt his back, and others had sustained injuries ranging from bruising and sprains to suspected fractures. She couldn't help thinking it was lucky that the carts were away and she had secured the galley just before, as it could have been worse if she hadn't. The crew had done a marvellous job with the medical kits; Olivia's arm was splinted and secured in place which had helped with the pain no end. With no life-threatening injuries amongst the dozen or so wounded it had been decided to continue onto New York, being that they were halfway between London and there, and flying over the North Atlantic when it had happened. It made sense to get them all to where the majority of passengers needed to be, and the injured ones would have access to quality medical facilities there. The passengers had been impressed at how the girls who had been serving them dinner just a little time before were highly qualified first aiders, and very competent ones at that. Olivia wished that she had been able to help them, she wasn't good at being a patient.

Eight hours later Olivia thanked the bellman who had kindly helped her up to her room with her case. He wished her well and closed the door gently. She winced as she tried to take off her jacket, letting it fall down her good arm. She was grateful for the small button on her short blouse sleeve that would come in handy when she tried to get it off over her cast in a minute. Her forearm had been fractured as she had suspected, and although the hospital were happy to release her back to the comfort of her hotel room the airline's medical assistance company advised she wasn't to fly home for at least forty-eight hours. The plaster cast felt heavy and awkward, but at least the drugs had helped with the pain for now, and she was so exhausted she doubted anything would keep her awake.

She took her phone and charger from her handbag and plugged it in next to the bed. Adrian had notified the company what had happened but she had declined his kind offer to phone her loved ones as she wanted to do that herself when she knew exactly what damage she had done. Only her phone had been out of charge when she was at the hospital, and now it was the early hours of the morning at home. After the way things had been left, she wasn't sure that Tom would care anyway but she would call him, right after she had a quick nap, she thought, as she laid on the bed still in her uniform and closed her eyes.

It was her phone ringing that woke her, and when she reached out to find it on the bedside cabinet the weight of the cast and the pain in her arm reminded her of the recent events. She looked at the clock, it was 2pm; she had been asleep for hours.

No caller ID displayed on the screen and she debated whether to answer it, grateful that she did when it turned out to be her manager back in the UK. He apologised for waking her and asked how she was, if she needed anything, and she thanked him for his concern. What she really needed was an unbroken arm and a good night's sleep, both of which were beyond his job description.

She hung up the phone and took a moment to think about what she was going to say before calling Tom. At least she had an icebreaker to take the conversation away from what had happened. The phone rang and rang but Tom didn't pick up, which wasn't unusual but surely on a Sunday he wasn't busy?

Won't be back tonight, had an accident on board and have broken my arm xxx, she texted, leaving enough information out to give him room for questions. She dialled the next number on her favourites list and her mum answered straight away. It was funny how talking to her mum made her feel like a little girl again, and tears trickled down her face as she told her about what had happened on the plane, suddenly feeling sorry for herself. She couldn't bring herself to mention what had happened with Tom though, as that would have meant admitting what she had done, and she was quite sure even her mum would frown on her for her actions.

'How long will you be off work for?'

Olivia hadn't even thought about that and tried to recall if anything had been said by any of the doctors.

'I've no idea Mum, I guess until this cast is off in a few weeks.'

'Well you need to come and stay for a while if that's the case.'

'Yes I will Mum, that sounds lovely.' It really did.

As she hung up the phone she opened the Facebook app, more out of habit than any need to see what anyone had been up to. She scrolled down through the Saturday night photos and the pictures of children and dogs, and the occasional mindfulness post. Suddenly something caught her eye and she sat bolt upright as she tried to process what she was seeing.

Sarah was looking back at her from the screen, pouting. Her low-cut top, or dress perhaps as it didn't show below her top half, showed off her long neck and cleavage, and her hair framed her face, falling perfectly either side. There was no one else tagged in the photo nor was there anyone else in it, but she could tell exactly where she was by the pool table that was clear in the distance and the jukebox which sat behind her, she was in HER den.

Olivia tried to calm herself, searching for an explanation. Of course she could have taken a selfie whilst she was there Friday night, but as much as she wanted that to be the case she knew that it wasn't.

Olivia pictured Sarah when she had arrived that night and she was definitely not wearing that same top, she was certain of it. Ok, she thought, it could have been innocent, she had found another reason just to pop by, but why had she been in the den again? Olivia could make out the rim of a glass in the bottom of the picture so it looked like she had stayed long enough for a drink, perhaps she had stayed for a few.

Olivia tried to call Tom again but still no answer.

Chapter 38

It was probably a good thing that Tom didn't call her back for two hours as it had given her time to calm down. She had finally managed to get out of the uniform and take a bath, conscious of not getting her cast wet. She hated that she was stuck here when she needed to be at home getting some control back in her life.

'What happened, are you ok?' Tom sounded concerned but distant at the same time, like he was only asking because it was the right thing to do. She wondered if he was still mad at her or if something else had happened?

Olivia told him about the turbulence and the fall, and all about the hospital. She needed to bring up the photo but didn't know how.

'Anyway, enough about me. How has your weekend been?' There it was.

'Just a quiet one, nothing much. Went to the office yesterday.'

Ok, she had two choices, she thought. She could carry on with this line of questioning, to which he would probably continue lying. Of course, he wasn't going to offer the information about Sarah being there, but she hoped he wouldn't lie blatantly when given the right question.

'Did you do anything last night?'

'No, just stayed in,' he said, matter-of-factly.

'Did anyone come round?' She knew Tom wasn't a great liar and she took his momentary silence as him trying to decide what to say.

'Not really.' He sounded under pressure, as if he sensed that Olivia already knew and she felt bad for making him squirm. There was no point in making him lie anymore, it wouldn't help anything.

'Sarah posted a picture of herself in the den so I presumed she had come over, again.' She tried to sound calm, as if she didn't have a problem with it.

'Oh, yeah, she left her purse here Friday so she swung by for it,' he stuttered, trying to sound as if he had just remembered. 'She stopped and had a drink, that was all.'

She looked a bit dressed up for someone who was just 'swinging by', thought Olivia. Was Tom really so naive?

'Did she stay long?' Olivia asked. She was treading a fine line, she knew, between innocent questioning and inflammatory comments that would make Tom mad again.

'No, no, not long. Anyway, when are you coming back?' he asked, changing the subject.

When she hung up Olivia mulled over the conversation; something didn't sit right with her. Based on the argument before she had left she had expected Tom to get mad, or defensive, when she questioned him about Sarah coming over, but he hadn't, he had just played it down. Perhaps he was beginning to see how insecure she was about her and was trying to save her feelings, being nice about it after all. She hoped that was the case. Maybe if they carried on in this direction he would be open to her suggesting letting Sarah go one day soon? But no, why had he changed overnight? He had been so mad before, and why had he offered her a drink, again, when he knew how Olivia felt?

Tom I find it really hard to see pictures of Sarah in our home when I am stuck here. You will probably never understand as you are not me, but I find her threatening and whilst I trust you implicitly there is something about her I don't trust. I am sorry, I know you won't want to hear this, but I hope you can try to understand and consider my feelings, please don't invite her in again when I am not there xxxxx

She pressed the send button and immediately regretted it, Tom would be furious. When her phone beeped she couldn't bring herself to open his message for a moment, scared of what it might say.

It's ok, I understand, sorry that she posted that, and that it made you feel bad, it won't happen again. Love you xxxxx

Olivia exhaled and felt relief washing over her. Finally, he was listening to her, she could talk to him, she wouldn't have to feel insecure anymore now that he understood.

As she came through the doors after customs two days later her face lit up when she saw Tom standing there behind the barrier with a huge bunch of flowers. Despite the sea of people they could have been the only two in the arrivals hall and she rushed to him, pulling her small suitcase with her good arm. Olivia breathed in deeply as he hugged her, so happy to be back in his arms, and she felt like everything was going to be ok now, they could get on with the rest of their lives. She had six weeks off now, and a plan, by the time she went back to work she wanted Sarah out of their lives and a ring on her finger. She was taking her life back and Sarah wasn't in her future.

Chapter 39

Honkers Bonkers, missing you Olivia. the photo of her friends on their night out made Olivia sad; she had missed the trip because of this wretched arm. Olivia had never broken a bone before and had not anticipated how much of a pain it would be, getting in the way of so many things you take for granted. She scrolled through their pictures, all typical night-time shots of them in Lan Kwai Fong having a blast. She recognised some of the other crew and pilots wearing inane smiles, bodies contorted as they danced to the music. A pretty blonde woman stood in the background of a few of the shots, watching with a big smile on her face as the crew acted as crew always did. She was either new, or she wasn't crew at all, thought Olivia. Either way she was obviously highly amused but not quite able to let her own hair down quite as much.

She had been home for two weeks now, and couldn't drive so was unable to go out much, and just popping into the office was not possible unless she took a taxi. Tom had been so lovely though, and hadn't mentioned Sarah to her once so she was in her happy little bubble where the Aussie minx didn't even exist. Well most of the time anyway, there was always that niggling feeling at the back of her mind. She typed her name into the search bar of Facebook, not knowing what she expected to find, but her last post was the one in her den so there was nothing new to worry about.

She had four weeks left to execute her plan, so she had better start soon. She picked up the phone and rang their favourite restaurant, booking a table for that evening. It was Friday, after all. If Tom wasn't intending to pop the question any time soon then maybe he needed a gentle push in that direction, a passing comment over dinner, a seed planted.

She called Tom's phone to let him know, forgetting about his calls being diverted, and reeled when she heard Sarah's voice.

Her days of being friendly and making small talk with this girl were over; she needed to know Olivia had no time for her. Surely she would move on if she knew she wasn't wanted? Perhaps Tom wasn't giving off the same vibes though, being the nice guy as always, she thought resignedly.

'Sarah could you tell Tom that I've booked a table at Puccini's for 8pm please?' she asked, politely, but that was all.

'Sure, no problem, will do,' Sarah replied rather more cheerfully, which just grated on Olivia.

'Thank you.' Olivia hung up the phone and headed for the shower. She longed to have one without the rubber bag that covered her cast getting in the way. It was almost five o'clock, Tom was always home by seven, and she wanted to look a million dollars by then, albeit a million dollars with a plaster cast, she groaned inwardly.

Seven o'clock came and went, as did seven thirty, and Olivia topped up her wine glass as she looked in the mirror on the living room wall. Her earrings sparkled, the diamonds that Tom had given her on their first anniversary, and she hoped she would have more soon. She had chosen a flattering black dress that hugged her figure and showed off all of the curves that she knew Tom loved, finished off with her favourite designer heels. Where was he?

She called his number but it went straight to answerphone; the office would be closed now so even Sarah wasn't picking up.

Where are you, the table is booked for 8! she texted.

A moment later Tom called back.

'What table, babe? I didn't know you'd booked anything.' He sounded flustered, like he really had no idea.

'I booked Puccini's,' Olivia said, deflated. 'I left a message.' *With Sarah,* she nearly added but it didn't need to be said.

'Oh babe, I'm so sorry.'

'Where are you?' she asked, hoping he could get home soon.

'In Croydon. Someone left a message to say there was a problem at one of the sites and I just had to pop up. I was going to call you on my way back in a minute. Bloody waste of time though, there was no one here when I got here so it couldn't have been that urgent,' he complained.

Well that was that, he wouldn't be home for at least an hour and by the time he showered it would be nine o'clock.

Funny, she thought, how he got that message and not the one from her. She fumed as she realised what Sarah had done, *the bitch!!*

By the time Tom got home all thoughts of a romantic evening were gone, Olivia consumed with anger at what she was almost sure Sarah had done. But she had no proof and she didn't dare voice it. She wasn't normally one to post anything on social media but she smiled at the camera with Tom for a selfie and put it up. *Romantic night in with this one*, she added as a caption, making sure she had cropped out the takeaway pizza boxes that were on the coffee table. She knew that Sarah would see it and she wanted her to see that her plan hadn't worked, even if it had.

Chapter 40

Sarah looked at the photo of the two of them and smiled to herself. Obviously the romantic dinner hadn't come off she congratulated herself. She sat in her car and watched as the lights in Tom's house turned off, because that was whose it was – Tom's. Olivia was just there for now, but she would be there herself soon enough, entertaining in the den and sleeping next to her gorgeous man at night.

It had been so easy, that night. Tom was so sweet he didn't question why she would have left her purse there, and when she had suggested they have a whisky he was too polite to refuse. She had an inkling that something had happened between him and Olivia because he didn't want to talk about her, which was fine by Sarah. It was probably just a minor row like couples have, but it had given her the opportunity she had hoped for, to reel him in when his guard was down.

The thing about men was that no matter how much they tried to be good, and faithful, ultimately they were still led by the animal part of their brain, and if you can lose the sensible bits they have no resistance to temptation. Sarah had perfected her skills with many men before, and although she had thought Tom might have been out of reach, or perhaps she had liked Olivia enough not to try, she couldn't resist the challenge.

The right songs on the jukebox, the banter as she beat him at a game of pool, and the bottle of aged single malt had warmed things up nicely, and when she saw that her prey was weak she had pounced. Tom hadn't been able to resist, he wasn't in control of his mind, and he had wanted her, she knew it. He had made love to her passionately, almost aggressively, Olivia thousands of miles away from him both in body and mind.

It was like he woke up though, when they came up from the den. She had thought they would go to bed but suddenly he had changed his mind, and seemed to regret it. She had seen this behaviour before too, and knew just how to play it. She hugged him and told him it was ok, that it had been a moment of madness and that she wouldn't tell anyone; she couldn't let herself become the enemy. This was just the beginning and the game had yet to play out.

As the last light went out Sarah started her car and began the short drive home. It had been a pain having Olivia home all this time. Tom was too available to her, and when she was home like this she was too forefront in his mind for Sarah to find a road in. She had behaved herself for two weeks now; Tom had hardly been able to look at her for the first few days but now the awkwardness was subsiding and he had started to soften towards her again, trusting her to keep her promise of silence. It would soon be time for her to make her next move, she just had to be ready as soon as an opportunity arose, or she created one.

Chapter 41

The train pulled out of the station and Olivia waved to Tom who stood stiffly on the platform, waving back at her quickly lest he look too girly, she observed, amused. He pulled his coat around him and folded his arms in defence of the winds that were howling across the station. As he disappeared from her view she sank back into her seat, feeling contented as she began her journey to her mum's.

They had finally managed to go for the meal at Puccini's last night. The restaurant never failed to disappoint and the atmosphere had provided the romance and level of *amour* that she had hoped it would. As they had shared the dessert and the waiter had topped up their wine glasses again, the timing had been perfect for Olivia to broach the subject of their future together. The ambience hadn't been wasted on Tom either, and he had been happy to talk about it, saying things were nearly in place, he just needed to fulfil this new contract successfully so that it would be renewed and then he would relax. Olivia doubted it, she knew him too well, but she loved him for his drive and ambition. She had jokingly told him she wouldn't wait forever, as she had had lots of other offers for consideration and he had laughed, promising that he would make a decent woman of her soon enough. For now she was happy with that, trying not to let her mind run away with wedding dresses and table plans, but she wasn't sure how long she could stand waiting for. She couldn't push it any more though, and all good things come to those who wait, she thought. Perhaps she wouldn't have a ring by the time she went back to work in three weeks but at least he had all but promised she would have one soon enough, so part one of her plan was almost successful.

Her mind wandered to the other half of her plan, to get rid of Sarah, and she looked around her for inspiration. So far she hadn't been able to come up with anything that wouldn't create an argument, and that would be counterproductive, but there must be something that would work.

She gazed absentmindedly at the hedgerows as they whizzed by her window, empty fields stretching behind them as far as the eye could see. A couple of houses, then more began to line the tracks, and she looked in interest at the gardens and windows, getting a glimpse into the lives of the strangers that lived there. Washing on lines, toys and trampolines, football flags hanging in windows, all belonging to people she would probably never meet, all with their own worlds to which they were central and Olivia was the stranger, the inanimate one.

That was it, she thought as the train slowed down,

pulling into the next station. To get Sarah out she needed to know more about her. She realised in that moment that she really didn't know her at all, and apart from Fiona's brief introduction at the barbecue she had never asked much more. She thought back to Sarah's social media page, with its lack of personal information. She mulled over the times in the office when she and Keira had been speaking openly about their pasts and realised how Sarah had never contributed, never offered anything up. She wondered if she was hiding anything, or perhaps she was just overthinking things now, but the suspicion was compelling. She suddenly wished she wasn't going away for the week; she wanted to begin her detective work right away, but she would have to wait, she told herself firmly. The facts, if there were any, would still be there when she got back.

Chapter 42

Sarah was pleased with herself. She had suggested to Tom that since the contract was due for renewal in just a few short months that it may be prudent to build stronger relationships with the men at the council, particularly Ted Coulter, who was the one with the final say on who won the contracts there. Tom had been impressed, having not thought of that himself, and had given her the go-ahead to sort something, arrange a meal to thank him for his custom.

Of course, she hadn't realised Olivia was away that week; she hadn't really overheard his conversation with Pete about her going to her mum's. She also wasn't to know that Puccini's was their special restaurant. Tom wouldn't remember about the message he never got a couple of weeks back.

Dear Sarah,

My wife and I would be delighted to accept Tom's very kind offer and very much look forward to the evening.

Regards

Ted

'Tom, I have booked you all into Puccini's Friday at seven. Ted and his wife are really looking forward to it, and meeting Olivia.' She smiled, standing at the door to his office innocently.

'Oh wow! That's great, Sarah, well done.' He looked nervous at the thought of it, out of his comfort zone entertaining powerful people. 'I hope I can think of enough things to talk about.' He looked up at her worriedly.

'You'll be fine, Olivia will be there to help you out.' She waited for the penny to drop.

'Oh shit.' His jaw dropped and he looked from side to side. 'She's away until next week.'

'Oh no.' Sarah feigned a surprised look, and put her hand up to her mouth. 'I'm so sorry, Tom, I didn't realise.'

'Oh it's not your fault. I'll have to go on my own I guess, but what the hell will I talk to his wife about? Shoes?'

She smirked at his sarcasm. 'Shall I say you can't make it now? Rearrange for another day?'

'No, I can't mess him around.' She watched his face as he processed the options in his head. She could see the mental struggle he was having, knowing there was only one solution and knowing it was probably a bad idea, for him. 'Sarah, would you mind coming with me? At least you can talk to both of them, and I know you're good with this sort of thing.'

'Of course, no problem. I did have plans for Friday,' she lied, 'but nothing I can't cancel.'

'Are you sure?' His forehead wrinkled as his smiled gratefully and raised his eyebrows at the same time.

'Yeah, happy to help, kind of my fault anyway.'

'No it's not, but thank you Sarah, I really appreciate it.'

She could feel Tom watching her as she regaled Ted and his wife with humorous stories. They laughed at her animated recounts of work-related disasters and how some things were done so differently in her homeland. She had watched Tom struggle to make small talk, and once the subject of the current contract had been exhausted she had seen he needed her. She knew she was good. Olivia may have been able to talk about travelling but she would have been far out of her depth with any business talk. She knew that Tom was admiring her, she could feel it. His body language changed as the evening progressed and she instinctively knew that he was back within her reach.

By the time that Ted and his wife left the four of them bade farewell as if they were old friends. Tom was euphoric, knowing that Sarah had achieved untold things and he couldn't hide his gratitude as he hugged her outside of the restaurant.

'We need to celebrate,' he declared in theatrical insobriety.

'The next contract is in the bag,' she declared, high fiving him.

The taxi journey was short, and their joviality didn't diminish by the time it pulled up at Sarah's.

'One last drink to celebrate?' She nudged him with

her elbow and grinned enthusiastically.

Tom was still in his hedonistic state and sat forward quickly, handing a ten-pound note to the driver, cancelling the next stop on the journey which would have taken him home, alone.

As Tom made love to Sarah that night she knew that she had him. It wasn't rushed and passionate, borne out of an argument with Olivia, this time he appreciated her. She had felt him all night, watching her, unable to control the attraction, the admiration, and he had finally succumbed. She was far more than Olivia could ever be to him; he needed her, and not only in that moment. As he had caressed every part of her body, they had bonded in ecstasy, lost in each other and afterwards his arms had felt *so* good around her as she drifted off to sleep, pleased with her accomplishment.

Chapter 43

Olivia loved being back with her mum, finding comfort in everything, from her childhood bedroom to the meals her mum was still cooking from those days. They watched soap operas together each evening and visited the family that were still living in the same houses they always had during the day, catching up with their lives and dramas. She spent time with her niece and nephew, marvelling at how big Oscar the gecko had grown on his diet of crickets. A week was enough though, she was beginning to feel like she was living in one of the soap operas they all watched, all thriving on the dramas that were an inherent part of village life. She boarded the train at Southampton Central, this time waving to the whole clan that had come to see her off. Her mum looked sad despite the smile and Olivia blew her a kiss, mouthing that she would 'be back soon.'

She was keen to get home; she had struggled all week to hold back on the urge to start her investigations. She knew she needed to do things right, not rush in all guns blazing and become the pariah in it all. She had to be discreet and gather any facts that she may find before she made any noises. It was less than two weeks until her first flight back, and she had set herself the deadline that she was going by.

Party at ours Friday, 7pm

She texted the message to Sam, Fiona and Lin. They hadn't had a good party for a while. She knew without asking that Tom would be up for it, and since she didn't have any flights it was the perfect opportunity. The fact that Fiona may know a thing or two about Sarah was just an added bonus. As they each texted back to confirm they would be coming Olivia felt things slotting into place.

Tom had been a bit quiet the past couple of days since she got back, but she had just put it down to work and pressure. After their meal she was still in the happy bubble waiting patiently for her promised future. She had been preoccupied herself by the anticipation of the party, busy making sure things were perfectly set up to ensure everyone enjoyed themselves.

As Tom let the last of their guests in Olivia descended down into the den carrying the canapés she had picked up that afternoon, placing them onto the bar. She had pretty much forgotten about her arm; the cast was just a bit of an annoyance now but she had become quite accomplished with her good arm and the limited use of her other hand.

The tray of champagne glasses were quickly filled with the Veuve that had been chilling in the ice bucket this past hour, and glasses were raised in toast to friends and good times. She was happy to see Tom relax and enjoy himself, and as the music got louder Olivia topped up everyone's glasses, playing the perfect host. No one seemed to notice that she was not topping her own up half as often as theirs.

As Fiona sat on the barstool, resting her feet after dancing to the last song, Olivia joined her, sensing her opportunity.

'Do you hear much from Sarah now, Fiona?'

'No, barely anything since she moved into her own flat. Is she still at Tom's?'

'Yeah, she's been a godsend to him, what with all the experience with her dad. I should have invited her tonight, I just didn't think. Remind me how you knew her again?'

'My old school friend Melanie. She and her family emigrated when we were about eleven but we always stayed in touch. Her brother Bill was a bit older, and he settled down quite quick with an Australian girl. Sarah was their daughter.'

'I wonder what made her come here. She doesn't really talk about it much, only really mentions her dad's firm but that's all, she's a bit of a closed book,' Olivia said casually.

'You're right, she didn't open up to us much either,' Fiona agreed, obviously happy to continue with the line of conversation, much to Olivia's pleasure. 'I got the impression something had happened and she had needed a break, probably had a bit of a break-up or something maybe.'

Now this was exactly what Olivia had been hoping for, a bit of a lead. So something had happened. She doubted Sarah had had her heart broken though, doubted it very much.

'Oh, the poor thing.' Olivia hated being so fake but needs must. 'Did Melanie not tell you anything?'

'No, I didn't ask her to be honest, so busy with kids and stuff I never gave it a thought.'

'Maybe it would be good to know. I can't help feeling she is lonely here, doesn't really have any friends. Me and my friend have tried, taken her out, but it just seems like she doesn't want to let anyone close, and don't tell anyone but she was really throwing herself at the men. I'd love to help her out if there is anything I can do, she's such a sweet girl.'

'You're so lovely Olivia,' Fiona slurred as Olivia handed her a fresh drink from behind the bar. 'You're right, I'm supposed to be looking out for her but I've been so wrapped up in my own life I have just let her get on with it.'

'Maybe next time you get a chance ask Melanie if Sarah is happy here, tell her we are a bit worried. I'm sure if she thinks you need to know anything she will tell you.'

'Fab idea, I will definitely do that.' Fiona raised her glass. Olivia poured herself a double measure of rum; her job for tonight was done, now time to enjoy herself.

'Let's dance!' She pulled Fiona up from her seat as one of her favourite songs came on the jukebox.

Chapter 44

Well she hadn't quite achieved what she had planned to in her time off, but at least she was making progress. Olivia sat on the bus from the car park to the terminal, and looked at her phone. She hadn't heard from Fiona since the party; she had obviously forgotten their conversation, understandably after the amount of alcohol that had gone down that night. She hadn't wanted to push things too quickly, but a week had passed now so it wouldn't look too suspicious, she thought. She felt bad about lying to Fiona about her concern for Sarah, but they weren't close enough friends for her to feel she could confide in her about it, and her loyalties may lay with Melanie.

Hi Fiona, just wondered if you had had a chance to speak to Melanie yet? Still keen to help Sarah out and can't help feeling she's sad at the moment. It was only 9am but she was sure Fiona would be up by now, probably just dropping the children to school.

Truth was Olivia hadn't seen Sarah; she wouldn't have known whether she was sad happy or whatever. The week had flown by between hospital appointments, getting her cast removed and being signed back fit to fly. She felt a little uneasy coming back to work after so long off, feeling almost new again, but she knew that by the time she landed into Washington it would be as if she had never been away. She rubbed her arm through her jacket sleeve – it felt strange without the cast that she had grown used to.

The bus pulled up outside Terminal 2 and she waited as all the security agents, engineers and various airport workers got off, before getting up and pulling her cabin bag down from the luggage rack.

'Thank you,' she called to the driver as she stepped down from the bus, and she smiled at the crew waiting to get on, recognising some of them. Despite them all still looking lovely in their uniforms she could always notice the slight paleness of the crew that had just flown through the night in their metal tube, deprived of natural light and sleep, and with less oxygen in their blood than others had.

As her belongings arrived out of the scanner in the staff security search ten minutes later she heard her phone ping.

Oh yes, completely forgot, sorry! Will definitely speak to her in the next few days xxx. Olivia could feel the anticipation, hoping her friend would unearth something she could use.

'I'm really sorry Olivia but can you speak to the passengers in 56 and 57K please? I can't deal with them any more.' Paul looked drained. 'It's the usual seat recline issue.'

Olivia rolled her eyes and sighed. So many times she had had to say the same thing to passengers.

'Madam, the lady is within her rights to recline her seat; you can recline your own to compensate for it.' The lady in front of her sat with her eyes closed and seat fully reclined as the aggrieved shook her seat furiously. It was not possible that she was asleep, she was just refusing to communicate any further.

'I want to complain.'

'Certainly, madam, but what is your complaint and where would you like to address it?'

'About her,' she shook the seat in front of her again, 'and to the airline of course.'

'But the lady isn't an employee, madam. The airline have no responsibility for her actions, and like I said, she is entitled to recline her seat.' Olivia wished the flight wasn't full and that she could move one of them to end the petty squabble. 'Now I'm sure she is a reasonable lady and that if you talk to each other sensibly you can reach a compromise.' The lady in front opened her eyes and nodded.

'If she had asked me nicely in the first place rather than shaking my seat I would have put it up a bit,' she said, looking at Olivia with a stern face.

'Well I am sure she would greatly appreciate it if you could.' Olivia looked at the other lady, who nodded but clearly couldn't bring herself to say anything nice or polite.

As the seat moved forward Olivia stood up from her crouched position. 'Lovely, thank you.' She smiled at the one in front. 'All sorted, I hope you are more comfortable now,' she said sincerely to the one behind, who nodded sulkily. It wasn't what she wanted to say to them, but in this job she often had to hold back what she truly wanted to say.

'Give me strength.' She walked back into the galley and Paul looked at her apologetically.

'I'm so sorry, I couldn't deal with them, they were like two children.'

'It's fine, hon, it's what I'm here for. Flying does strange things to people.' She wondered if the lady behind was perhaps a little anxious, claustrophobic maybe, and that was why she had acted that way; often there was more to it when people were extremely unreasonable. Olivia was always the first one to give someone the benefit of the doubt, look for the good.

The plane wobbled, a little bit of mild turbulence, and Olivia's heart raced. For a moment she felt anxious herself, and as the flight smoothed out moments later she noticed she was holding onto the galley side with all her strength. For a while she had forgotten about her last flight but it was obviously still on her mind and she would probably be nervous of turbulence for some time she thought.

'Right, let's get this last service ready.' She shook herself off and focussed back on the task at hand.

Olivia felt amazing as she jogged steadily along the path that ran alongside the river and into the centre of Washington DC. She hadn't run for the whole time she had been in plaster and it felt good to feel the breeze against her skin as her music pumped through her headphones. She smiled at strangers running past her in the opposite direction and she felt almost euphoric as the voice on her running app told her she had completed 5k. Now she just needed to get back, she thought, as she turned into West Potomac Park.

She sat on the steps of the Lincoln memorial, looking down along the reflecting pool and up to the Washington Monument obelisk that stood proudly at the far end. She loved the clarity she felt in her mind at times like this; no other job would give her the chance to sit peacefully at such an iconic place and just think. She mulled over the past few weeks, trying not to get hung up on Sarah, worrying for a moment that she was getting obsessed. Looking around her, breathing in the tranquillity of the place, she felt calm and contented. Her mind cleared and in that moment she hoped that Fiona wouldn't unturn anything, that it would all just go away. She would let it all go, just avoid Sarah and stop obsessing. She didn't like how she had been acting, it wasn't the person she really was, and Sarah would move on eventually anyway, she was sure.

She breathed in deeply and stood up, taking it all in, before beginning the run back, starting with the steps down from her resting place. It was a quick turnaround and the wake-up call was booked for 5am local. The sun was beginning to set in the distance as she jogged back to the hotel, happy in her own mind.

Chapter 45

Sarah stared at the stick, trying to work out what she was seeing. Surely it was a mistake. She couldn't be pregnant, could she? Tom had used a condom every time they had made love, he had insisted. She felt her stomach lurch and her heart thud in her chest as she remembered Ethan, she had been so drunk, she couldn't remember if he had been careful. She sat on the sofa and her thoughts collided noisily in her mind. What the hell was she going to do?

Since the meal there had been more times. Tom couldn't see past his desire now, couldn't think with his head. Men were all the same. He had connected with her that night, and now his body was drawn to her, and he couldn't resist the urges. She almost felt bad for him when he expressed his guilt over Olivia, announcing each time that it couldn't happen again, that his future was with Olivia. Then why was he making love to her? Why was it her that was laid naked across his desk, again, as he devoured her? She had wondered when the push would come, she had to remain dignified and a good person, but eventually he would have to choose, and she certainly wasn't intending on making it easy for him.

She looked at the blue cross again. Maybe this was it. She wasn't averse to having a baby, although she had thought it would be later in life, and planned. Tom had everything she needed though and could give her a good life, so maybe this was meant to be. Nobody knew about Ethan, and nobody ever would.

'I have to get off.'

Olivia looked at the sheer terror in the girl's eyes as she pleaded with her to let her off the plane. Everyone had boarded and the pilots had just signed the final paperwork ready for departure. The last member of ground staff stood next to her at the boarding door and Olivia could read her thoughts. *Please don't get off, please, you have no idea how much work that will create for me*, or something very similar to that.

'Madam, honestly, you will be absolutely fine. All of us have been flying for years and have never had anything bad happen.' *Apart from falling down the stairs,* she thought, but decided against sharing.

'I can't, I'm so sorry, I thought I could do it but I can't.' Tears sprung from her eyes and rolled down her face. Olivia wanted to hug her but instead rubbed her arm gently. She couldn't force her, they couldn't take the poor thing hostage, and she was travelling alone so there was no one else to take responsibility for her.

'Come with me.' Even the ground staff lady sounded a little sympathetic despite the fact that she would now have to locate her suitcase in the hold and reissue the paperwork.

As was often the case, one problem led to another, and in the time it took to locate the suitcase, which couldn't be on the plane without the owner, they missed their take-off slot. The airport was crazily busy and another one couldn't be allocated for ninety minutes. The crew did their best, giving out drinks and trying to help those with tight connections, but it was what it was. Some would have to stay overnight at Heathrow now and hope their onward airlines could get them away the next day. Such was aviation, things didn't always run smoothly.

'I want to get off.'

For a moment Olivia couldn't process what she heard; it was like an echo, a previous event repeating itself. She turned to see a tall man in his fifties glaring at her, with a backpack slung over his shoulder.

'I'm gonna miss my connection so I'm getting off,' he declared in a soft southern drawl.

'But sir, we are due to leave in just twenty minutes, I'm sure you can make it.'

'No ma'am, I only had two hours so I'm sure to miss it, therefore I'm off.'

'Do you have baggage in the hold?' She crossed her fingers and hoped that he didn't.

'Sure do.' His face was deadpan; he knew what he wanted to do and he was going to do it.

'Sir, I can't make you stay onboard, but if you get off now it could delay us significantly more, and these poor people want to get home,' she pleaded with him.

'I don't give a rat's ass about people I don't even know, miss, now get me my bag and I'll be on my way.' He thrust his baggage receipt at her and stepped off the aircraft onto the jetbridge. The ground staff lady stopped in her tracks as she turned into the jetty clutching the new paperwork, and looked despairingly at the man standing off the aircraft. Olivia held up her hands, hunching her shoulders to signal she couldn't do anything about it, the man knew his rights and was quite clear that he wasn't for reasoning with.

The ensuing delay stretched the six-and-a-half-hour flight time to over ten hours, and with the time from checking in to pulling up at their gate in Heathrow, the crew were almost out of hours. It was dark and the roads were empty as Olivia drove home, feeling quite exhausted. They had still had to deliver all of the services once they took off, leaving little time for a break in such a long day. At least she could go home though, she consoled herself, unlike some of the poor people who were now trying to find somewhere to stay after missing their connections.

Olivia climbed into bed quietly, wrapping her arm around Tom's warm sleeping body. It was good to be back.

Chapter 46

Something was a matter with Tom, she knew it, but whenever she asked him he just said that it was nothing. He had been like this since she got back from Washington three days ago, seeming worried, and she could only assume it was about work. He probably didn't want to concern her, she told herself, or maybe he thought she wouldn't understand. So she stopped asking and just tried to support him, making him nice lunches each day and showing him lots of affection in the way of cuddles and so forth. He wasn't interested in sex though. She had never known him to be like that, but she didn't force things, hoping that whatever it was that was worrying him would be sorted soon. Maybe she would have pushed him for answers if he was being grumpy with her as a result, but he wasn't, quite the opposite in fact, telling her constantly how much he loved her. At least there was a positive side to his strange mood, and if it wasn't affecting her adversely she would just go with it.

Flights came and went in the ensuing two weeks, Los Angeles and San Diego, and still Tom acted strangely when she was home. She couldn't fathom it, he was almost clingy, like he was afraid he was going to lose her, but surely he knew that no matter what, even if heaven forbid the business failed, she would still love him?

She wasn't helping in the office now so she didn't know what the problem could be, but she had decided that seeing Sarah made her unsettled so she chose to avoid the situation. Fiona had messaged to say her friend wasn't aware of any problems, that Sarah was always a little bit of a loner, and Olivia was happy to just move on now, dropping her obsession.

It had come to the crunch now though, and as she pulled into the gravel car park for the first time in weeks she was determined to get to the bottom of what was worrying him. She had watched him pacing up and down that morning in the kitchen, looking at his phone and rubbing his face. He hadn't known she was there, managing a fake smile when she walked into the room, before hugging her and heading off. Maybe she would have to ask Sarah if Tom wouldn't tell her. Maybe she would know what was troubling him.

No one was in the front office when she opened the door, so she knocked gently on the door of Tom's. Sarah opened it and her face dropped when she saw it was Olivia standing there. She said nothing, looking back at Tom who was leaning against the window. She wondered what they had been talking about; the atmosphere was thick and she could feel the gravity in the air.

'Everything ok?' she asked, looking from Sarah to Tom.

Tom straightened himself. 'Olivia, what are you doing here?' he asked, trying to sound carefree but failing miserably.

'I bought you some lunch, you skipped breakfast.' She held up the bag she was carrying, her decoy, the reason she needed just to pop by.

'Thanks babe.' He walked over and took the bag from her.

Sarah hadn't moved, she was just stood there watching Tom. Olivia wondered if they had fallen out; there was definitely something between them.

'Sarah, I need to speak to Tom, alone.' She didn't say it meanly, but Sarah looked back at her defiantly and then at Tom.

'Sarah, please.' He gestured for her to leave, almost pleadingly, and she closed the door loudly behind her.

'What the hell is wrong with her?' Olivia asked.

'No idea, I'll never understand women,' he quipped, not making eye contact.

'Tom, I need to know what's going on.'

For a moment she thought she saw a look of panic flash across his eyes, but it was gone before she could be really sure.

'What do you mean?'

'Oh, Tom, stop it, stop telling me there's nothing wrong. I'm not stupid, I know you. You can tell me what it is, if things are going wrong here you can be honest you know, I'll still love you even if you are bankrupt!' She smiled, although she meant it she hoped it wasn't that serious, she had grown accustomed to her comfortable life.

Tom laughed, not a full belly laugh, but he was obviously amused, and he looked a little relieved, she thought. She was glad to see him lighten up a bit.

'Oh babe, I'm not going bankrupt!' He wrapped his arms around her and kissed her head. 'But it's nice to know you would stay with me even if I was.'

'So what is it, Tom? I need to know. I watch you worrying, I know something is up. Are there problems here?'

He held onto her, so she couldn't see his face. 'Just a problem with one of the contracts, babe, but I'm sorting it, nothing for you to worry about.'

She pulled herself back and looked at him seriously. 'Ok, but you can talk to me you know. I might not know a lot about the business but I'm a good listener.'

'Thanks. I do love you, Olivia.'

'I know you do. Don't be late tonight,' she said as Tom opened the door to let her out. 'I'm cooking your favourite.' She turned and kissed him.

Sarah coughed, reminding Olivia that she was there. 'Hey Olivia, did Tom tell you my news?'

'No,' she replied, hoping that it was about her leaving.

'I'm pregnant,' she smiled. 'I can't believe you didn't tell her, Tom.'

'Oh yeah, sorry I just forgot. Anyway I really need to get on.' He placed his hand in the small of Olivia's back and gently pushed her towards the door. Olivia was so shocked by Sarah's news that she hadn't noticed the colour drain from Tom's face or the smug look on Sarah's.

'Um, congratulations,' she called over her shoulder, already at the door with Tom practically pulling her out of it on the pretence of walking her to her car.

'Sorry babe, I'm really up to my neck in it, I've got to get on, thanks so much for the lunch.' He kissed her and turned back to the office. Olivia got into her car dazed and a little confused, trying to process what had just happened. So Sarah was pregnant, that must mean she had a man, and that would mean a long maternity leave coming up soon too. Bingo! She grinned broadly as she drove out of the yard.

Chapter 47

'Tom, I think you need a break. Come to New York with me this weekend,' she suggested as they sat either end of the sofa after dinner. 'Before you say you can't, it checks in late Friday so you can go into work in the morning, and gets back Sunday night. Pete can cover for you if anything comes up.'

'That would be great.'

She hadn't expected it to be that easy, thinking he would need a lot more persuasion being the workaholic he had been these past months.

'Fabulous, I'll book your ticket now!' She got up to get the laptop, excited now about her next flight.

It couldn't have worked out better. The flight was wide open with lots of empty seats, and Tom had been allocated one in First Class, not bad for a £140 standby ticket.

'Your drink, sir.' She placed a whisky down on his table and winked. She didn't want to upset the other passengers, who had paid thousands for the same seats, so she had to be discreet. Tom looked so relaxed now that he was away from it all, like his worries had been left in England. He smiled back at her gratefully. She wasn't working in this cabin but she had just wanted to make sure he was ok, and she returned back through the curtain to economy, pleased that her idea had worked.

'Phone,' Olivia demanded, holding out her hand. Tom was just about to open the hotel room door as they headed out the next morning, turning back and looking at her with a confused, maybe worried expression.

'Huh?'

'You are leaving your phone here. It's Saturday, and we are going to have a nice day. I'm fed up of people keep messaging you, and you worrying. This was meant to be a break.' Tom's phone had been beeping since he arrived, and even when he had put it on silent she knew he was checking it in the bathroom and when he thought she was asleep. Surely nothing could be that important Pete couldn't deal with it. 'I mean it,' she said in her best school teacher voice.

He reluctantly handed it to her, just as another message came through and the screen lit up. Tom grabbed it so fast she didn't have time to read the message, but she *had* seen who it was from, it was from Sarah.

'What the hell does she want? Surely she's not in on a Saturday.'

'Um, yeah, she was popping in to catch up on some stuff, just needed to know where something is,' he stumbled. He quickly typed a reply and turned the phone off this time, before walking over and putting it in the safe himself. Olivia had never been a snooper, it had never even crossed her mind to check Tom's phone, but for a moment she felt an overwhelming curiosity. Perhaps if she had a quick look when she got a chance then she could get a better idea of what was worrying him lately. It couldn't hurt, she would be doing it with best intentions. She instantly scolded herself. How could she even consider it? You didn't do things like that. What was wrong with her? Tom finished typing the code into the safe keypad and walked back to the door.

'Right, let's go, no more calls.' He seemed relieved.

New York City never failed to disappoint. They strolled through Central Park and then along Fifth Avenue, with its designer stores and huge skyscrapers. Tom carried Olivia's bags dutifully, encouraging her to buy whatever she wanted, within reason of course, and she didn't need to be persuaded. They, or rather Olivia, marvelled at the rings in Tiffany's, hinting somewhat unsubtly at the designs that she liked, making sure that he was clear on her tastes.

They posed for selfies at the top of the Empire State Building, spending an age looking out over this vast city, in awe of the buildings that really did scrape the sky. Central Park, in its autumnal colours stretched out in the middle, a picture of calm that contrasted with the buildings looming over it on all sides. They strolled along Broadway and as dusk settled over the city they looked around for somewhere to eat.

'I wish we didn't have to go home tomorrow,' sighed Olivia. They sat in the window of the restaurant that revolved at the top of the Marriott in Times Square, passing the famous buildings, trying to place them on the map that was printed on their cocktail napkins. Olivia's shopping bags spilled out from under the table into the floor area around them.

'Me too,' Tom agreed. Olivia could see he really meant it.

'I hope things get better at work soon, I hate seeing you under all this pressure.'

'I'll sort it out, I promise. You don't deserve the way I have been.' He was looking out blankly into the city and Olivia thought he looked sad.

'Come on, no moping, we only have tonight and we need to make the most of it.' She signalled for the waiter who was passing.

'Can I get a bottle of champagne please?'

For the rest of the night there were no worries; they laughed and chatted like they hadn't a care in the world. When they got back to the hotel they made love and it was like it used to be, before Tom had changed, but he was still there and she hoped he would be back for good soon. His phone stayed firmly locked away until they left the next day, and even then he didn't turn it on.

'Did you have a nice time?' asked the captain as they came down to reception to check out.

'Lovely, thanks,' replied Olivia.

'Yeah, really nice,' agreed Tom, 'we should do this more often.' He smiled at Olivia.

'Shame about the loads, but the jumpseat's yours if you want it.'

Olivia looked at the captain, puzzled.

'There's about fifty spare, isn't there?'

'No, I don't know what happened, I think one of the flights got cancelled so we are full now.'

'Oh!' Olivia hadn't thought to check the loads again. Thank goodness she was the only one with a companion as there was only one spare jumpseat on this aircraft, which they could use if the captain said so. 'Thank you so much, that was a close one! Sorry babe,' she apologised to Tom.

'No worries, can't complain, I'm happy to stay here if I have to,' he joked.

The joys of standby travel, thought Olivia, but she knew Tom would be ok, it was only six hours, and it was a day flight, a couple of films on his iPad and they'd be there. At least he was getting on.

Chapter 48

It was amazing, she thought, how the black cloud had descended back over Tom's head as soon as they touched down in London. She watched him getting off of the plane from where she stood at her door, looking down at his phone with that look of concern that was so often on his face lately. She sighed inwardly; at least they had had a brief moment together when things were ok. She hoped it was enough to carry him through the week and the troubles he bore. She wondered if things were too much for him, if he had taken on too much, but he had always coped before, working hard and keeping a level head. When he slept that night she couldn't resist the urge, and reached over to where his phone laid next to the bed. It was pin locked though, and after two failed attempts she sighed as she put it back. No answers were to be found there. Just as she drifted off it rang, the cheerful jingle confusing her momentarily.

'Hello?' Tom's groggy greeting sounded equally confused. Silence. She could make out a voice but not what was being said, and Tom quickly moved into the en-suite. He probably presumed that she was asleep and didn't want to wake her. Moments later he was putting on the clothes that he had just hours before deposited on the bedroom floor.

'What's up?' Olivia sat up and switched on her bedside lamp.

'Oh, sorry I woke you. It's nothing. Go back to sleep, babe.' His pale face told her that it wasn't just nothing.

'Where are you going? It's two o'clock in the morning.' She confirmed it, looking at the time on her alarm clock.

'Oh just work, babe, I'll explain later, gotta go.' He kissed her and rushed out of the door before she could ask him any more questions. She racked her brains trying to think of what could possibly have happened in Tom's line of work that would call him out at this time. He wasn't an emergency service, surely whatever it was could have waited until the morning? Oh well, she thought, as she lay back down and switched the light out, she wasn't going to get any sort of explanation now so she would just have to go back to sleep, and she liked sleeping.

Olivia woke up in a cold sweat. The dream was so vivid. Tom was in serious trouble, trapped in a hospital room with a crazy doctor, strapped to the bed, screaming in terror. She couldn't get the door open, didn't know the code, and was watching helplessly through the glass window as he came towards Tom with a huge knife. Where the hell did that come from? She felt the clamminess of her chest and exhaled in relief that it was just a dream, albeit a bad one.

Instinctively she reached for her phone and called Tom's number. It diverted to the office but no one answered and the voicemail kicked in. She hung up and looked at the time, midday, surely someone, namely Sarah, should be there by now?

Call me, she texted him, hoping he would pick it up soon and call her back. The dream left her worried; she couldn't help feeling he was in trouble, not that she had ever thought her dreams had meaning before, but perhaps this one was just bringing her real worries to life.

'Sorry babe, you wouldn't believe the day I have had.' Tom walked in the door, a little after seven. Olivia had been beside herself with worry and was ready to scream at him for his selfishness, until she saw the huge bouquet of flowers that he was carrying. He handed them to her with the sweetest look on his face and she couldn't be angry with him anymore.

'I've been so worried. Why didn't you return my calls?'

'I'm so sorry, I had to turn my phone off in a meeting and I forgot to turn it back on again.'

'And what was the emergency?'

'Oh, it was just some tiles fell off the roof at the school site, had to fix it up quick before the kids got there for school this morning.' He looked down at the floor, taking his shoes off with his spare hand. Olivia reached out and took the flowers off of him, admiring their beauty.

'At two o'clock? Who was there at that time?' She

couldn't grasp it, didn't quite buy it.

'They have security guards that do patrols through the night, they must've phoned the caretaker and he called me. Anyway, what's with all the questions? I've had a long day and I was just looking forward to spending the evening with my beautiful girl.'

She gave in. He was right. Why was she asking so many questions? Why didn't she just take his word for it? She studied his face; there was something different. He looked tired, yes, but he looked lighter, like that dark cloud that had been following him around for weeks had finally moved away.

As they lay in bed wrapped in each other's arms Olivia couldn't help thinking over the day. 'I tried to call you but there was no one in the office. Was Sarah not in today?'

She thought she detected his body stiffen slightly.

'No, she was sick. She won't be working for me anymore.'

In her mind Olivia heard the celebration, corks popping, people cheering, music playing. It was all she could do to stop herself jumping out of bed and dancing around the room.

'Oh really? Why?' She tried to hide the excitement in her voice, glad that he couldn't see her face.

'Oh, it's not been working out for a while so I had to let her go. Keira is going to come back a bit early though so it's all good.' She thought that she heard in his voice that he was pleased that Sarah was gone too.

Chapter 49

'Olivia, will you marry me?'

Olivia felt light-headed, worrying for a moment that she might faint. Tom was down on one knee holding an open box with the most beautiful ring she had ever seen in it. The diamonds sparkled, reflecting the sunlight that streamed through the window of the restaurant that he had taken her to in Brighton. No matter how many times she had pictured this moment, she could never have anticipated the emotions she would feel, tears flowing as she nodded her head, unable to speak. Tom stood up to the cheers of the other diners, bowing in embarrassment, hating the attention, but he was a traditional man at heart and had to do things the right way.

Olivia stood and threw her arms around his neck. She didn't care that everyone was watching them, she was the happiest girl in the world right now and she wanted them all to see it. She cupped Tom's beautiful face in her hands and kissed him, locking this moment in her memory forever.

When Tom left the table later to use the restroom

Olivia couldn't stop herself taking a photo of her new gift, posting it straight to her timeline for everyone to see; she knew that they would all be so happy for her. She quickly texted her nearest family so that they could feel like they were the first to know. She suspected her Mum might be hurt if she heard it through someone else. The messages of congratulations were already flowing in by the time Tom returned, she even had one from Sarah, and she was glad that there were no bad feelings. She didn't show Tom though, not knowing really what had happened there, and not wanted to tarnish this moment.

They finished their perfect afternoon with a walk along the pebbled beach, wind blowing Olivia's hair furiously around her face. Tom held her hand tightly and listened as she babbled about how she would like the wedding; she had so much to organise. She kept looking at him, checking that he was not looking panicked. She didn't want him stressed again. It had only been a week since they had got back from New York, but he seemed more than happy to listen to her excited rambling.

She was still excited as they drove home, calling her mum, her sister, Claire, she needed them to be in this with her.

'I can't believe I am finally going to be your wife,' she said softly, looking at Tom as they drove into their road. 'I can't wait.' She had finally calmed down and now all she felt was pure unadulterated happiness.

Tom glance back at her and smiled. 'Neither can I.'

He indicated to turn into their house, clicking the control to open the gates.

'What's that?' Olivia leaned forward in her seat trying to make out what the object was that appeared to be hanging from the handle on the gate as it opened.

Tom looked too, and as they pulled up alongside it Olivia saw that it was a child's doll, a baby doll.

'Weird,' she said, trying to work out what it could be doing there. 'Are you ok? Tom?' Tom looked like he had seen a ghost; all the colour had drained from his skin and he was staring at the doll.

'Yeah, yeah.' He shook his head vigorously. 'Sorry, I um, just felt a bit funny that's all. Yeah, you're right, that is weird.'

'Oh, I know,' Olivia smiled, pleased with herself for her deduction, 'some kid has obviously dropped it and the next person who had passed has put it there because it will be obvious if they come back looking for it.' She looked at Tom. He was nodding and the colour was returning to his face.

'Yes, that must be it. Freaky-looking thing though. If it's not gone tomorrow it's gonna have to go in the bin, I can't face that every time I come home.'

They both laughed, driving on through and closing the gates behind them with the doll still attached. If they had looked back as the gates shut they would have seen Sarah step out from the shadows of the trees opposite.

Sarah looked across the road at the doll, still hanging

on the gate. She hoped that Tom knew it was her, that it hurt him. Their baby was gone, lost, but surely she needed more support than she had got.

Yes, Tom had come to the hospital when she called that night, and she could see he was affected by it too, as far as he knew it was his child she was losing. It should have made him care for her, want to look after her, but no, he had waited until she woke up from her procedure and told her that it was over. He had been torn apart, not knowing what to do when she was pregnant, but now that she wasn't anymore it would be easier for them just to stop seeing each other completely. He would pay her for another month, like she should be grateful, she seethed. She had no job, no boyfriend, and no baby.

She hated him, and she hated Olivia, posting those dumb photos of her ring, lapping up the congratulations, living in her perfect house with her perfect boyfriend. Well she had no idea, and there was no way Sarah was going to let them just carry on with their perfect lives while she was left with nothing.

She felt the rage boiling inside her, her lips pursed and she breathed heavily. He had no idea what he had done. *No one* gets away with treating Sarah Fischer like that.

Chapter 50

'Right, doing it now, requesting Hong Kong 11th January.' Olivia tapped the details into the bid page. 'Can't flippin' wait.'

'Try not to fall down any stairs between now and then,' said her friend dryly.

'I will wrap myself in bubble wrap, I promise,' she laughed. It was only early November so she was going to have to take great care for the next couple of months! 'Are Ali and Nicola requesting it too?'

'Of course,' replied Claire, 'and Julie Margot wants to come with us.'

'Really? How'd that happen?' Olivia asked in amusement.

'I bumped into her at check-in on my last flight and she was asking after all of you. I just mentioned we might all do a Hong Kong together and the next minute she's coming with us! You don't mind, do you?'

'Of course not, at least we know we'll get decent breaks.'

'And she'll definitely be up for coming out, could be amusing.' The girls giggled and the subject quickly changed back to the impending wedding. Nothing had even been booked yet, but it was sure to be the main topic of conversation between now and whenever the date would be.

At least an hour passed before Olivia suddenly realised what the time was. 'Gotta go, babe, gym class booked in half hour.'

'No worries, speak soon, love you,' replied Claire as she put down the phone on the other end.

Olivia just made it, running into the class with a minute to spare. She quickly set up her step and bar at the back of the room, relieved that there was any space for her as this class was always full.

'Right, anyone here never done my class before?' asked David the instructor with an inane grin, looking around the room. They all looked at each other; it was always the same faces, and they knew what was coming next. An arm reached up in the far left, second row back. David looked over at the new victim with a menacing smile. 'Well this is *extreme* legs, bums, and tums,' he told her. Olivia felt sorry for the new girl, she remembered how hard she had found these classes when she first started.

As the music blared and Olivia pushed herself through the punishing routines she glanced occasionally over to her, watching to see how she was faring. She admired her determination, only seeing her stop to retie her blonde ponytail; she was obviously quite fit.

Forty minutes later, as they lay on their mats in sweaty messes, Olivia looked up as one of the girls from the front row tiptoed quietly out of the room.

'Right, cobra positions, ladies,' directed David.

As Olivia lifted her head up she studied the faces in the mirror that stretched along the front of the hall. Now that the person from the front had moved she could see the new girl's face for the first time, and she almost lost her balance as she realised who it was. What on earth was she doing here? And surely it was a bit of a tough class to do in her condition?

'Thank you, ladies, see you next week.' David's words took a moment to register through the sound of her heart pumping in her ears. Olivia rushed to get the weights off of her bar, wanting to get them away and get out of there before she had to face her. She hoped that Sarah hadn't seen her but as she stood impatiently waiting to hang her mat up she felt the hairs on the back of her neck stand up and she knew that she was right behind her.

'Hi Olivia.' Olivia had hoped that she would never have to hear that voice again. She wanted to ignore her, just walk away, but she couldn't, her conscience wouldn't let her. Despite everything, despite her dislike for the girl, she hadn't actually done anything really wrong to her, and she felt a pang of compassion, wondering if she was ok now that Tom had let her go. She turned slowly.

'Oh!' she feigned surprise. 'Sarah, fancy seeing you here, I didn't know that you came to this gym.' She tried to smile, but knew it wasn't sincere.

'I just started, thought it must be good if you came

here.'

Olivia tried to quickly process what Sarah was saying. Was she saying she came here because she knew Olivia did? Surely not. She felt uncomfortable, grateful as she reached the stand and hung her mat.

'Wasn't it a bit hard in your condition?' Olivia said quietly, looking down at Sarah's incredibly flat stomach.

'Oh, no, I lost the baby, and things didn't work out with the dad.' Sarah rubbed her tummy, looking away momentarily.

'Oh, sorry to hear that.' And she was, but she fought her urge to ask more. 'Sorry Sarah, I really have to go.' She didn't want to get into conversation, even though she did want to know more. She wondered how Sarah knew she came here, trying to remember if she had ever mentioned it to her. She wanted to know what had happened at the office, and how she was getting on now, but for once Olivia restrained herself from asking, not sure she really wanted to know the answers.

'Oh, that's a shame, I was hoping we could grab a coffee and catch up.' Sarah smiled sweetly at her. Olivia kept walking towards the exit, but Sarah stayed firmly by her side. 'Please let me buy you a drink, I could really do with talking to you, Olivia.'

Chapter 51

This was a bad idea, Olivia told herself, sitting at the table waiting for Sarah to bring over the drinks, wondering how on earth she had been talked into it, why she couldn't have just said no. The coffee shop was quiet, people sat in their wooden chairs, scrolling through their phones as they sipped their drinks, or chatting quietly between themselves. An old man sat with his dog in the window, and Olivia wondered if he was lonely, if he had anyone waiting at home for him, any family to visit. She watched Sarah at the tills, and felt her guard drop as she wondered the same about her.

'One skinny latte.' Sarah put Olivia's drink down in front of her, and sat down in the chair opposite, opening her bottle of water. 'Thanks for coming, Olivia.'

'That's ok, I don't have long though, a lot to do today.' She sipped her latte, grateful that it wasn't too hot and wouldn't take too long to drink.

'Congratulations on the engagement, you must be stoked.'

Olivia rubbed her engagement ring and smiled. 'Yes, I am, thanks.' She knew Sarah wanted her to ask her how she was, but she just couldn't.

'Tell Tom I am really happy for you both.'

'I will, thank you.' Olivia took another large sip.

'And can you tell him I've got a new job, so he doesn't have to worry. I know he felt bad about the way things finished.'

How? thought Olivia. *How did they finish?* She looked at Sarah, wondering if she could read her face, if she knew that Olivia didn't really know what had happened, hoping she would give her something, but still unable to ask. She waited but nothing came, just silence.

'Well that's good news.' Olivia was the first to speak. 'Anything good?' She didn't see that this question could hurt.

'Yes, actually, I'm going to be the PA for Ted Coulter.' She must have seen Olivia's blank expression. 'At the council, the one who deals with Tom's contract.'

Olivia gulped her drink down, looking at her watch but not seeing the time. 'Well that's good news Sarah, I am sure you'll love it there.' So not only was she now at her gym, but she was still involved with Tom too. Why couldn't she just disappear? 'I really do have to go now, I have an appointment,' she lied.

'Oh, ok.' Sarah looked sad. 'It's been really lovely to talk to you, Olivia, I don't get to talk to girlfriends very often.' Olivia watched as she hung her head, hand on her stomach, and wondered what she had been through. She couldn't imagine how Sarah had gone through losing a baby and breaking up with the father without a girlfriend to talk to.

'Don't you have any friends you can talk to, Sarah?' She felt sorry for her.

'No, not really, I didn't really have any at home. I think I told you I was home schooled, and I haven't really made any here except you, I only met builders at Tom's.' She looked up sadly at Olivia.

Olivia sank back into the chair. She knew she was beaten, that she couldn't possibly just walk away now, that Sarah needed her. Why, oh why, oh why did she have to care? Why was a Sarah *her* problem? But she couldn't just leave her, the girl needed a friend, and for now Olivia couldn't see anyone else lining up for the position.

Two hours later Olivia walked back through her front door, mentally exhausted. She didn't want to be doing this, didn't want to be Sarah's friend and counsellor, but she didn't have anyone else, so how could she walk away? She was so young, dealing with all of this all on her own. She put her gym bag down in the hallway and walked through the kitchen, placing the pile of letters she had just taken out of the post box onto the side. Opening the fridge, she took out the bottle of wine that was standing in the fridge door, and poured herself a large glass.

She sank into her sofa with her phone and mindlessly began scrolling through her newsfeed. A notification flashed up, and she clicked on it, probably someone's birthday or something unimportant as it usually was.

Sarah Fischer has tagged you in a post.

A photo of them on their night out was on the screen, she remembered Sarah asking Claire to take it. *Thank you for being such a good friend*, it said underneath. Olivia rolled her eyes and took a gulp of her wine, moving past the post swiftly, not commenting on it. She heard Tom's keys in the door and turned the phone off. Enough of that for tonight now that her fiancé was home. She smiled.

Chapter 52

What was in that envelope that had affected Tom? One minute they had been clearing up in the kitchen together, happy, and the next minute Tom had looked like he'd been punched in the stomach, leaving the room clutching the envelope and the letter that he had just taken from it. Olivia looked through the other letters that still lay scattered on the side; no clues as to what had just upset him were to be found there. She finished putting away the plates, walking out of the kitchen wondering where he had gone.

Five minutes passed slowly, Tom not replying to her calls, although she hadn't shouted in case he was on the phone. Eventually he appeared from the den, with no sign of the letter, and a look on his face that she couldn't quite read.

'Are you ok?'

'Yeah, yeah, fine. Sorry, just had to make a quick call.'

'What was the letter about?' she asked casually.

'Nothing, nosey,' he teased, walking back into the kitchen.

Olivia wondered if he was really allowed secrets anymore now that they were getting married. Surely she was entitled to know everything now. Oh well, maybe she didn't want to know everything really, it would probably only bore her if it was about work anyway!

'I saw Sarah today,' she called over her shoulder. No answer. 'Did you hear me, Tom?'

'Oh, yeah.' He sounded distracted.

'She said to tell you she's got a job with Ted Coulter and congratulations on our engagement.'

'Oh.'

'She's joined my gym.' Nothing. 'Tom.'

'Sorry babe, I have to go out.' Tom walked past her quickly, car keys in hand. He looked almost angry, she thought, not looking at her as he headed for the front door.

'Where are you going?' Olivia asked, confused.

'I left something at the office, won't be too long.' And that was that, the door closed and he had gone.

Olivia sat bemused on the sofa; he had been so much better lately but things were going weird again. *Oh well,* she thought, topping up her glass, *I'm sure it's nothing serious.* She picked up her phone and typed 'wedding dresses' into the search bar of her browser.

She was soon lost in the pages of fabulous dresses, screenshotting all of her favourites, and laughing out loud at the ridiculousness of some. Maybe she would take her mum to New York and look at the dresses in Vera Wang. She had been to the store on Madison Avenue once before with another crew member, and could remember vividly the rows of beautiful silk and lace dresses, and how stunning the girl had looked in the ones she had tried on. She had hoped then that it would be her turn one day, and now it was here. She giggled as she pictured her mum's face when she saw the price tags, and how she would assure her that she didn't have to worry, she wasn't expecting her to pay for it. Despite tradition, she knew Tom would be happy to pay for things, and it wasn't as if there was a father-of-the-bride anyway, sad for a moment when she realised her dad wouldn't be there to walk her down the aisle. The sound of the doorbell dragged her back from her self-loathing and back into the room.

That was strange, she thought, that someone was ringing the bell but hadn't buzzed the gates first. Tom must have misplaced his front door key. She opened the door, but no one was there and Olivia was puzzled as she looked out into the driveway. The lamp that hung by the door threw light in an arc around the front of the house but darkness shrouded the edges and Olivia couldn't see into the shadows. She thought for a moment that she heard a rustle near the bushes on the left, and she shivered uneasily. It must have been a cat, she thought, as she closed the door quickly, although whilst that would explain the rustling it didn't explain the doorbell. She was pretty sure that was beyond the abilities of most felines.

Suddenly Olivia felt uneasy; she had a feeling that she didn't recognise at first, hadn't felt for many years, maybe since childhood – *fear*. Quickly she went to the back of the house and checked that the back door was locked, terrified now that someone was in the garden. She pulled the curtains hastily to shut out the shadows outside that seemed to be moving, sitting back on the sofa, drawing her legs up to her chest. She called Tom's phone but there was no answer. *Damn him for going out,* she thought. The doorbell rang again and Olivia wanted to scream, the fear was turning to terror and she tried to wake herself up. If only she were really asleep, she wished.

'Hello?' she called shakily, loud enough so that if anyone was at the door they would hear. The bell rang again. 'Hello?' Olivia called again. She could hear her voice shaking.

Olivia crept up the stairs, trying not to make a sound, and made her way into the front bedroom. She hid behind the curtains as she peered down into the driveway. She couldn't see anyone, but a small brown box sat on the floor in front of the door. The light had gone out, not having detected any motion for some time, and Olivia stood deathly still, her senses heightened as she watched for anything that would explain what was happening.

Chapter 53

Fifteen minutes had passed and nothing had moved. Olivia's heart rate was beginning to slow down. She left her position to check through the back windows; nothing was in the garden that she could see. Tom still wasn't answering his phone as she came back downstairs and walked tentatively to the front door.

The box sat there innocently, but Olivia still approached it with caution. She was torn between grabbing it quickly and running back inside, or treating it like it might be a bomb. *Get a grip, girl. Who the hell would leave a bomb on your doorstep?* she mocked herself, picking it up, looking around her and retreating swiftly behind the safety of the door.

Placing it gently on the kitchen side she studied the box. It was a little smaller than a shoebox, but square in shape, taped shut on all sides. It looked innocent now, a harmless present left by someone who didn't want to be seen – a surprise. She tried Tom's phone one last time, not wanting to open it on her own.

'Sorry babe, I left my phone in the car. I'm on my way back, are you ok?'

Olivia was so relieved to hear his voice, and tried to stop the tears that threatened to fall as she told him about what had happened.

'Don't open it until I get there,' Tom ordered her.

'It's ok Tom, I don't think it's a bomb,' she said, trying to sound braver than she really felt.

'I know, but some weirdo has left it on the doorstep and run off so I don't want you opening it on your own, ok?'

'Ok,' agreed Olivia, not wanting to open it on her own either.

'I'll be five minutes.'

Olivia felt the relief wash over her as she heard the gates open and Tom's car pull in. He came through the door moments later, and she looked up at him from where she sat and couldn't help but let the tears flow. Tom wrapped her in his arms and held her tightly as she sobbed, letting all the emotion of the last hour leave her.

'It's ok now, I'm back,' he reassured her.

Once she had calmed down he released his hold and cupped her face in his hands, wiping away the last of the tears.

'Right, where is it?' he asked gently. Olivia gestured towards the kitchen. Tom got up, and Olivia went to follow him.

'You stay here, you've had enough drama for one night.' As much as Olivia wanted to know what was in it, she did as she was told, grateful that he was looking after her.

She heard the sound of the tape being cut and the box being opened, before Tom gently closed the door. What on earth was inside it that he didn't want her to see? She heard the back door open and a minute or two later close again, then the sound of Tom walking back across the kitchen. The fridge door opened and she heard him exhale loudly as he took a bottle of beer from the shelf, before finally opening the door and coming back into the lounge.

'Must've been kids messing about, there was nothing but a clown toy in it,' he said reassuringly. There had been a film out in the cinema lately with a scary clown in it, so it was plausible, she thought, that kids would find this a funny way to terrify people. 'I've put it straight in the bin. I'll get someone around tomorrow to fit security cameras, I don't want you to worry.' He put his arm around her as he sat down; she loved that he cared so much and was comforted by his plan, wondering if she would ever feel quite the same again when she was on her own here.

'I had better go to bed,' Olivia said, noticing that it was almost eleven o'clock, 'I haven't even packed yet. Come up with me?' She looked at Tom pleadingly, not wanting to be on her own, still nervous. Tom drank the last of his beer from the bottle and got up, following her protectively.

Sarah was pleased with herself; her night had been a success. She waited in her car, the new one she had bought last week, and watched Tom drive back into his house. She had ignored all of his calls, and his angry voicemails saying that he was at her house. She had told him straight, in the letter, to leave Olivia or face the consequences.

It was simple, he would have to split up with Olivia either way, whether through his own choice, or because *she* made it happen herself. Sarah thought she had been quite nice about it up until now, offering herself to him, selling their new life together as a good alternative, but he just couldn't see it. She had even got the job at the council so that she could help him, *if* he was nice to her, or she could lose him the contract if he wasn't.

What was this hold Olivia had over him anyway? She really wasn't all that. Why did Tom have to still think with his head and his heart, instead of his dick, like most men? She was exasperated; he obviously needed decisions to be made for him, so she would have to split them up.

The box had been a bit impulsive admittedly, but she had been so angry after she had left Olivia. She had joined the gym without much of a plan, just knowing that she would be able to keep an eye on things if she were able to get Olivia to trust her. Olivia was weak, a goody-goody, and she knew she wouldn't be able to help herself being nice if she played on her weaknesses. She was right, it had been a pushover to get her to go for a drink, listen to her fake troubles, but she'd sat there in the coffee shop, rubbing her face in it, keeping on touching her ring, and playing with its big diamonds. Raging, she had stopped herself screaming that her life wasn't so bloody perfect, that Tom wanted to be with her really.

When she had seen that bride and groom model in

the card shop window afterwards she had bought it mindlessly. Back in her flat it had felt good to imagine that the bride in the model was that bitch, as she had dug out its plastic eyes and sawn its throat with a steak knife. She was so pleased with what she had done she needed Olivia to see it too, and so she had come up with the idea of leaving it on the doorstep for her. Luckily the walls weren't so high and she had managed to get over them without much trouble, and without being seen.

She smiled menacingly as she recalled the terrified way Olivia had called 'Hello?' too frightened to answer the door, as she had hidden in the bush, and tried to imagine what she had looked like when she opened the box, the pathetic cow that she was. She knew Tom would know it was her, but she hadn't done anything to the groom, so she hoped he would know she wasn't angry with him anymore, she couldn't stay angry with him for long.

Chapter 54

Olivia's phone beeped as she got out of the shower.

Your flight to Houston this morning is cancelled. You are stood down today, please acknowledge and check your roster for further updates.

Result, thought Olivia, grateful that she hadn't left the house yet. She sat on the bed and thought for a moment what she should do with her extra day off. Despite the urge to get back into bed she soon reached into her drawer and pulled out some gym clothes; there was a good spinning class at 9:30 that she could make if she hurried.

As she walked across the car park Olivia smiled, feeling invigorated. The worries of the night before had drained away as she had pedalled manically to the music and the shouts of the instructor. With every imaginary hill that she had climbed she had felt stronger, defiant, she wouldn't let the actions of some kids that she didn't even know make her a victim.

As she started up the car she nearly didn't notice

the piece of paper stuck under her windscreen wiper. She opened her door and reached around to remove it, tempted to throw it on the ground but stopping herself and put it on the passenger seat. It wasn't the first flier that she had had put on her car, never advertising anything that was of any interest to her. Surely they were a waste of the advertiser's time and money, she thought. As she sat in the line of cars exiting the car park she opened it absentmindedly, not really interested, but stopped when she noticed the handwriting. It wasn't a flier after all, it was a note.

Your boyfriend doesn't love you, he is only with you because he feels sorry for you. He is having an affair with someone better than you, you should leave him.

Olivia felt sick. The sound of the horn beeping from the car behind reminded her where she was and she dropped the note back on the seat as she started to drive. As she pulled up at the house what seemed like moments later she realised she had no recollection of how she had got there, that she couldn't remember any of the drive home. She picked the note back up and sat there in the car staring at it. It was definitely a girl's writing, she could tell by the loops and the way the letters flowed, but it looked like it had been written in a hurry, without much thought to the content. Who would write this? Was there any truth in it? Surely she would know if Tom was cheating. Surely he wouldn't have asked her to marry him if he didn't want to be with her. She felt the anxiety burning her chest, remembering the fear of the night before, and now the thought that someone had been watching her, seen her car and taken the time to put the note on it. Was it possible that the two things were connected? She tried to talk herself down, find the sensible explanation. It had been kids the night before, hadn't it? The note didn't mention a name so maybe it was just another weirdo playing some messed-up prank?

She hadn't noticed Tom's car parked there, maybe because he was never home during the day so she hadn't expected him to be now, and her mind was elsewhere. She looked over at it as she turned the key in the lock, still holding the note in her other hand. As she walked into the house she could hear him shouting. She didn't think she had ever heard Tom sound so angry before. He obviously hadn't heard her come in and she closed the door quietly, trying to hear what he was saying.

'You're mad, just leave us alone, it's over!' Silence, presumably as the object of his fury spoke. Olivia crept towards the kitchen where his voice was coming from. 'I swear to God, if you ever come anywhere near my home or me again I will call the police, I should have called them last night.' Olivia held her breath on the other side of the door, wishing for a moment that she hadn't heard anything, that her flight hadn't been cancelled and she wasn't stood here right now listening to her world fall apart. 'Sarah, you have to move on, it wasn't anything, we had nothing, it was all a mistake.' His voice was getting lower, he sounded desperate almost. 'I love Olivia, I will never leave her for you. Why can't you get that into your head?'

Olivia pushed the door open. Tom had his back to

her, his phone to his ear and other hand rubbing his head.

'Tom.' She couldn't say any more. She had no more words.

Tom froze momentarily before turning around slowly. He looked at her, like he was trying to tell how much she had heard, but it must have been clear that she had heard enough. He hung up the call, not looking at the phone or taking his eyes off of Olivia's face as he put it down on the side. Olivia stepped forward, looking at the object next to the phone, trying to work out what it was. Tom followed her gaze to the wedding figures that were sat there, but he moved too slowly to grab them and Olivia gasped as she saw the face of the bride, covering her mouth with her hands.

Olivia didn't know what to do, but she couldn't breathe and she needed to get out of there. She turned and walked hastily towards the front door, getting back into her car and driving, with no idea of where she was going.

Chapter 55

Olivia sat in her car at the side of a nameless street swinging frantically through her emotions. Tom's face flashed up time after time on her phone as he tried to call her but she couldn't pick up, she had nothing to say. She didn't want to call anyone as she didn't know what to tell them; she didn't know the full story herself yet, and she felt numb. She tried to replay what she had heard, hoping to realise that she had jumped to the wrong conclusion, but she knew there was no doubt. She kept hearing his voice. 'I love Olivia.' So why the hell had he slept with Sarah? *The baby. Oh my god, was it his?* she thought, realising how deep he had really been in. It wasn't just a one-night stand, it had been much more.

Please come home, we need to talk, I love you. Olivia read the text. Just words, his actions said otherwise.

As Olivia sat there her thoughts turned to Sarah, how she had sat in the coffee shop just the other day and reeled her in, all the time knowing that she was talking about Tom when she spoke about her lost baby's father. Anger came, replacing the numbness, and Olivia could feel her pulse speed up as she pictured Sarah's smug face. Then the mutilated face of the bride figure came into her mind and she shivered at the thought of Sarah disfiguring it whilst picturing her own face. Fear came fleetingly, taking her back to the night before and how the box was delivered, knowing now that Sarah had been the one hiding in the shadows, watching her. The lies, how Tom had told her it was a clown, that it was kids, when he had obviously known it was *her*. What other lies had he told?

Then came the sadness, and Olivia wept. She wept for what she knew she had lost and for the darkness that hung over her future. She wept for her memories that she was longer sure were real, and the tears flowed until she had none left. She couldn't go home, couldn't have that conversation, so she drove as the sun was setting and headed for home, to her mum, the only person in the world who she truly trusted right now to love her.

The next few days were a haze. Olivia's mum had opened her arms to her daughter and wrapped her up in a blanket of security, in the way that only mums could do. She hadn't pushed Olivia to tell her everything, just being there ready to listen to the bits that she would let out here and there. Tom had come knocking but she had sent him away, knowing instinctively that her daughter wasn't strong enough yet to face him, and telling him to be patient, that Olivia needed time. She slept a lot, trying to escape from reality, not wanting to think anymore, not knowing what to do.

Eventually the whirlwind slowed down in Olivia's mind and she started to see through the fog a little. After a week she knew she needed to go back, that she needed to face her demons, and she hugged her mum tightly as she said goodbye.

Tom was at home when she got there; he looked like a shell of himself and Olivia was surprised that she felt sorry for him. She listened as he told her the truth about what had happened, warning him not to leave anything out if they had any chance of overcoming this. She knew Sarah had manipulated him, that she had set out to get him and wasn't the sort to fail, but she couldn't believe he had had so little control. She had come back not knowing whether she could stay with him or not, and when she went to bed that night in the spare room she still didn't. She tried to process what he had told her, picturing them together in the den, and at Sarah's flat whilst she was away, oblivious. The lies since hurt her the most, and the fact that Sarah had *stalked* her, made her afraid, it all made it too hard to just put it all behind her.

When she got up in the morning Tom was out, and she sobbed again as she packed her things into suitcases, looking around at her home that felt so cold now, so tainted. She took off the engagement ring that had made her so happy such a short time ago and left it symbolically on her bedside table. She couldn't see a way forward and couldn't think here, she needed to be away for a while, to go through the grieving process.

Chapter 56

Over the next few weeks Olivia was thankful every day for her friend who had taken her in and given her her spare room without hesitation. For years she had been the one that Claire had leant on but now that she was the one who was broken her friend was there by her side, supporting her. Once the shock had subsided, and the pain had lessened, Olivia found herself consumed with anger. It was with her through every minute of her day, almost paralysing her as she thought of what Sarah had taken from her, and she couldn't shake it off.

Claire spoke to the airline and it was agreed that they could fly together for the next three months, a buddy roster so to speak, the idea of being on her own in a hotel room with nothing but her thoughts scaring Olivia. After two weeks off the girls chatted as they packed their cases for two nights in Los Angeles, and Olivia felt excited to be going away, leaving everything behind her.

'Can we leave a bit earlier? I need to stop off somewhere on the way.'

'Where?' Claire asked, intrigued.

Olivia couldn't bring herself to actually voice her plan, knowing that it would sound completely mad.

'You'll see,' she smirked.

Claire was still looking perplexed as Olivia came out of the pet shop with two carrier bags, looking completely out of place in her smart uniform, grinning wildly. Olivia put her purchases into the boot and hopped back into the driving seat.

'Are you going to tell me what you're up to?' asked her friend, still looking completely confused. Olivia just smiled and drove without saying a word.

As she pulled up outside of Sarah's flat she had a brief moment of uncertainty, quickly replaying her plan in her mind before deciding it was completely justified.

'Come with me.' Claire got out of the car and followed Olivia around to the back of the car. Olivia handed her one of the carrier bags and Claire recoiled when she looked inside.

'What the hell?' she exclaimed, Olivia just smiled again and walked quickly to the front of the building, pressing the tradesman button on the keypad to open the main door. Once inside she climbed the stairs swiftly, putting her bag down outside Sarah's door and signalling for her friend to follow. From the bags she took out one container of insects at a time, emptying the contents quickly and quietly through Sarah's letterbox. She tried not to laugh out loud at Claire's shocked face as the crickets, and the locusts fell through into Sarah's hallway. When all twenty-five tubs, each containing upwards of twenty creatures, were emptied the girls ran back out and jumped back into the car as if they had just robbed a bank.

As they turned out of the road they howled with laughter.

'You are absolutely mad!!' shrieked Claire, trying to catch her breath, holding her stomach.

Olivia explained how terrified Sarah was of bugs, and how it had come to her last night when she had spoken to her nephew on the phone about his gecko. The tears that ran down her face now were from laughing.

'Don't get mad…'

'Get even,' finished Claire.

Chapter 57

Olivia marvelled at how being busy at work made her feel normal for the first time since *it* happened. The flight was a typical LA, with its mix of hip music types, and the women whose faces were frozen with surgery, lips inflated, acting strangely as the champagne and Valium mixed in their systems. It was only as she lay in her bunk on her break that she shed a tear, getting up again when she realised that laying there was futile.

'You're back early,' said Steve, loading up boxes of hot snacks in the galley.

'I couldn't sleep, too much going on in my head.' Olivia tapped her right temple with her index finger.

As Steve loaded the snacks she told him how she had split up with Tom, giving him a brief lowdown on what had happened. They had flown once before, although neither could remember where, but for this flight they were like lifelong friends.

'Will you get back together do you think?' he asked earnestly.

'I don't know. I still love him but I don't think I can forgive him.' Olivia looked at the floor sadly.

'Time will make that easier, hun, it's up to him to earn your trust again though, but it sounds like he knows he made a big mistake so that's a start.'

'But how can I guarantee he won't make another one?'

'Haven't you ever been tempted by anyone else?'

Olivia shook her head mindlessly, but suddenly a brief memory of Jez flashed across her mind. She hadn't thought about it for so long she had forgotten that she too had been unfaithful that time. It was nowhere near on the same level of course, but how could she sit so high and mighty, judging Tom, when she wasn't perfect herself? She hadn't been tempted since, so perhaps Tom would be the same, perhaps there was hope.

'Olivia?'

'Sorry, I was just thinking, maybe you're right.'

Ding, a call bell went.

'I'll get it.' Olivia poked her head out to see where the call was from, taking a glass of water with her in anticipation of the request.

The lady sat in 47D scowled at Olivia, or at least she thought she was scowling, it was difficult to tell when her face didn't move. Her coral lipstick was smudged, spreading outside of the lines of her over-inflated lips, and her eyes had that look of being pulled back with the skin that had been stretched taut into her hairline. Her blonde hair was more than likely a wig, sitting too perfectly in a long bob considering how long they had been on the flight now. Olivia guessed she was about fifty, although the surgeries had left her looking much older, like someone seventy trying to look thirty again, the irony of a lot of the facelifts she had seen.

'Can I help you, madam?' Olivia asked, smiling, pleased that she could feel the movement in her own cheeks.

'I can't sit in this uncomfortable seat any longer, it is giving me back pain,' she said in her California drawl.

'Oh, well I'm sorry to hear that but unfortunately we are full today and I have nowhere to move you to, madam. Is there something wrong with the seat?'

'Everything, it's not fit for an animal,' she replied loudly, attracting the attention of everyone around her.

Olivia didn't have the patience, and walked away. Sometimes she could humour these people but today was not one of those days. Perhaps the lady should have booked a seat in first class if she had wanted something bigger and more comfortable.

Ding – the seatbelt signs came on.

'Ladies and gentlemen the captain has found it necessary to switch on the fasten seatbelt signs as we pass through this area of turbulence. Please return to your seats and fasten your seatbelts,' came Steve's voice over the PA. The plane shook slightly.

Olivia walked to the front of the cabin and started to check that the passengers had their seatbelts on.

'Excuse me, I told you I cannot sit in this seat any

longer, I insist you move me.' Olivia had reached row 47.

'Madam, I have told you I have nowhere to move you to, and since your seat doesn't appear to be broken there is nothing else I can do for you.'

'What's your name?'

'Olivia.' Olivia pointed to her name badge. Why did some people think that the fear of being reported would suddenly get them an upgrade or special treatment? Olivia carried on down the aisle.

'Secure on the left-hand side, Steve.'

'Thanks babe.'

'47D wants an upgrade, she isn't finding her seat comfortable enough.' They both rolled their eyes.

'No, missy, I am not.' Olivia froze, reading in Steve's face that the lady was stood right behind her.

'Madam, the seatbelt signs are on, please return to your seat,' said Steve firmly.

'Not until I speak to the captain about this,' she insisted. Olivia thought she detected a slur in her voice.

'Madam, I have told you twice now, I have nowhere to move you to.' Olivia had turned around to face the lady, trying her best to remain calm and professional.

The plane shook and the lady grabbed at the galley side to steady herself. Olivia wondered how much she had had to drink.

'I am sure you have somewhere in first class, you're just lying to me,' she spat, pointing her bony finger at Olivia.

'No, madam, I am not. We are full, and even if we weren't I couldn't upgrade you simply because you don't like the seat. Now please go and sit down.'

'I told you I don't like that seat and I will *not* sit in it any longer.'

Olivia looked to Steve, unsure in that moment exactly what she should do, wondering if she could possibly force the lady to go back.

'Madam,' said Steve slowly, 'I must ask you to comply with the captain's command to have your seatbelt fastened, now please go and sit down.' As he stepped forward to take her arm and guide her back she stepped back, looking as if he had just gone to attack her.

'Get the hell away from me, I'll have my lawyers on you if you so much as lay a finger on me.'

Olivia had always prided herself on her ability to be in control of her actions, a skill needed in her job, so she was shocked when she heard herself responding.

'Madam, return to your seat now and fasten your seatbelt, or we will have no choice but to have you met by the authorities when we land for being disruptive. There's nothing wrong with your effin' seat, now go and sit in it!'

The lady's jaw dropped, the most expression Olivia had seen on her face so far.

'I'm writing in a complaint, I can't believe you just said that to me.'

Olivia took a deep breath and said slowly, 'And

neither will the airline, madam.'

Steve pulled the curtain across the galley as they lady walked back to her seat, speechless. The shocked look on his face was replaced by a smile, followed by hysterical laughing.

'That is quite possibly the funniest thing I have heard anyone say to a passenger, ever!'

Olivia was caught between laughing and shock that she had said it herself, hoping that no one else had heard.

'Oh my god, you will tell them that I never said it if she writes in, won't you?' She looked at him pleadingly.

'Of course babe, it's her word against ours. Don't worry, she deserved it!'

'What's going on?' It was Claire down from her crew rest.

'I think I may have come back to work before I was ready to deal with these people,' Olivia replied, looking at Steve who was still pink-faced from laughing.

Chapter 58

The next day Olivia felt the happiest she had done for a long time. She, Claire and Steve hired out rollerblades and cruised along the path that ran along Venice Beach and up to Santa Monica. They took a break to admire the view at Muscle Beach, as the oiled and tanned weightlifters showed off to their audience, and again to watch the basketball match being played further down. They passed the vendors selling their indie wears from the stalls that lined the promenade, and the people sat outside the cafés and restaurants, all hoping to spot someone famous. Performers showed their skills, with crowds forming around the young boys spinning on their heads along to the music coming from their tinny speakers. For a long time she was so far away from home that it was like another universe, and she wasn't in it.

They arrived at Santa Monica Pier feeling a little weary, taking off their blades and putting their flats back on.

'Let's get lunch,' suggested Claire, not needing to persuade the others.

They walked up to the main street of shops, finding their favourite Italian restaurant, and requested a table outside. Despite it being late November the sun was still shining and the air was warm.

'Just popping to the loo,' said Claire, putting her bag on the seat.

'Me too,' said Steve. 'Are you ok to watch our stuff?'

'No probs,' said Olivia, sitting down in the seat next to the railings that separated the restaurant from the 3rd Street promenade.

She reached into her bag and took out her phone, taking the opportunity of being on her own for a moment to check it. Despite living apart she still needed to know that Tom missed her, that he still wanted her back, and his daily messages full of remorse and emotion helped her feel less alone with her pain.

As she looked at the screen she saw that Lindsey had tried to call her five times, and sent a message telling her to call her back urgently, all in the space of the last hour. Olivia tried to guess what on earth had happened as she dialled her friends number.

'Olivia, I've been trying to get hold of you!' Her friend sounded almost panicked. 'Someone set light to the office and they've lost everything.'

Suddenly Olivia was back in that world that had been so far away just moments away.

'Oh my god, are they ok?' Olivia tried not to panic.

'Yes, they are fine, there was no one in the office,

it happened a couple of hours ago after they had shut up.'

Olivia looked at her watch; it was two o'clock in the afternoon in California, so ten o'clock at home. She felt relieved that no one was hurt, but couldn't imagine how this would impact Tom and Pete.

'Is Tom there now?'

'Yes, they've just got back, do you want to speak to him?' Olivia wondered if Lindsey knew what had happened, she still hadn't told many people, holding back until she decided what to do. Her friend didn't wait for an answer.

'Olivia?' Tom's voice sounded shaky. 'Is that you?'

'Yes, are you ok?' Olivia asked softly. Despite everything she still cared deeply.

'Yeah, but it's all gone, all the paperwork, all the files, there's nothing left.' She could hear the despair in his voice.

'What happened?'

'We don't know yet, the inspectors are coming back tomorrow to have a proper look over it and see where the fire started, I just hope we are insured, and that everything was backed up.'

'Surely Keira was doing that?'

'Yes, but I am more worried about before she came back.' He didn't need to explain further, he meant Sarah, and it would mean getting back in touch with her to find out.

'Well I'm sorry to hear about it, but I'm glad you're ok.' Olivia felt her sympathy wane slightly as she thought of Sarah. Claire pulled out the seat and sat down opposite her. 'I have to go.'

'Ok.' Tom sounded sad. 'Olivia, I miss you.'

She wanted to say it back, because she missed him too, but the words wouldn't come out. She pressed the red button and ended the call.

'Everything ok?' her friend asked, and Olivia filled her in on what had happened.

'It's not your problem, hun, not your job to be there to support him anymore.'

Olivia wished she could be as strong as her friend wanted her to be.

'Right, shall I order the wine,' said Steve cheerily as he returned to the table.

'Yep,' replied Olivia without hesitation.

Olivia stared out of the window at the murky water of the Thames snaking through London. The view was amazing, without a cloud in the way, and she lost herself for a while as she spotted the landmarks that were dotted along the river. The Millennium Dome, the London Eye, Westminster, all stood so grand and imposing. Olivia wished that they would never land; she had felt so detached from it all these last few days, and enjoyed the trip so much.

The plane turned back towards the runway and as London's Finery disappeared behind them the city sprawled out to its boundaries. The motorway looked busy. she thought, before remembering that she was driving home with Claire so it didn't matter if it took a long time, she would have company. Perhaps it was the fact that she hadn't been on her own with her thoughts these last few days that had made her feel stronger.

The weary passengers shuffled slowly past Olivia at her door and she gave them a weak smile as she bade them farewell. She wondered how many of them were going back to their happy family lives, how many had no one, and she felt sad again. Her break was over and she had a feeling that the week ahead would be a difficult one.

Please call me as soon as you can. Tom's message appeared as soon as she turned her phone on. She put it back in her bag and boarded the bus to the car park with the rest of her crew that had driven to work.

'Bye girls,' waved Steve, heading off to the departures level to get his flight home to Sitges, near Barcelona. 'Come visit me soon!'

They both blew him kisses back, promising they would take him up on his offer in the near future.

Just landed, can't talk now. She texted him back quickly once she had sat down. Claire sat next to her, also tapping away on her phone, catching up with her own affairs.

Ok, can I see you later? Tom texted back immediately. She didn't know if she was ready, and she suspected that seeing him on landing day wasn't a good idea, but she couldn't help feeling sad for him, and wondering how he was.

I'll come round about 8, she replied, pressing send quickly before she changed her mind.

Thank you xxxxx

'Everything ok?' Claire must have heard her exhale loudly.

'I just agreed to see Tom tonight, I'm not sure it's a good idea on landing day.' She looked at her friend, needing her opinion.

'Probably not but get a sleep in now and see how you feel later.' Olivia was grateful that her friend wasn't too pushy, letting her make her own decisions, ready to pick up the pieces if it went wrong. They talked over things on the drive back, and Olivia knew by the time she climbed into bed for a nap that she would go over tonight, although she had no idea what she would say.

Chapter 59

It felt strange driving through those gates, and up to the house that didn't feel like her home anymore. She knocked the door, not feeling that she could use her key, and heard Tom's heavy footsteps approaching.

He looked awful. The dark circles that surrounded his eyes were testament to his lack of sleep, and his face looked drawn, almost gaunt. The numbness returned, masking any feelings that Olivia had, protecting her.

'Thanks for coming.' He looked so grateful, holding the door open for her. She could smell spices, like he had been cooking, which was confirmed moments later when he led her into the kitchen.

'I thought you might be hungry,' he said. In all of their time together Olivia had never known Tom to cook anything other than frozen food, but it smelt delicious, if only she were hungry. Two glasses sat on the side, and Tom poured wine into both, passing her one. Olivia's instinct was to say no, knowing the effects of alcohol on landing day, but she thought he looked broken enough that she didn't need to hurt him any more and took it graciously.

'How was your flight?' asked Tom, plating up the curry into two bowls and placing them on the table. She took a seat, wondering why she felt so uncomfortable.

'Good, thanks.'

Tom sat opposite her but didn't make any moves to eat his food.

'Olivia, I miss you. What can I say to make you come back? I'm so sorry.'

Olivia looked down at her plate.

'I don't know.' She didn't, that was the truth.

'I promise I will never ever look at another woman, I never did. I don't know what happened, it was like I wasn't in control, but I never even wanted it. I only ever wanted to be with you.'

Olivia thought he might cry, his eyes looked watery. Perhaps if it had just been once she could have forgiven him more easily, but it had been more and she didn't know if she could get past that.

'I don't know, Tom, I think I need more time. I don't know if I can forgive you.' She felt bad for a moment as she watched his face crumple. The tears rolled down his cheeks.

'I've lost everything.'

She had never seen a grown man sob before and she couldn't help herself getting up and holding him. He held her arm that she had wrapped around him as he sat in his chair, and wiped his tears away, trying to pull himself together.

'The office, it's all gone, and they think the fire was started deliberately.'

Olivia sat back down and looked at him, waiting for him to say more.

'They found traces of fuel, and reckon it looks like an arson attack. The police have sealed it off as a crime scene.'

'Who would have done it?' Olivia knew that Tom was thinking the same as her, but she couldn't quite believe it, that *she* would have gone that far.

'They wanted to know if I suspected anyone but I said no.'

'What?' Olivia felt anger rising.

'I don't know, I feel responsible. If it was her,' he clearly couldn't bring himself to say Sarah's name, 'then aren't I partly responsible for making her go crazy?'

Tom and his bloody morals, something she had once admired about him, but now it incensed her.

'No, Tom,' she said loudly, unable to hide her anger. 'Just because you fucked her doesn't mean she can burn down your office, or send that awful package for that matter. The girl is crazy.'

He nodded his head.

'You're right, I will tell them tomorrow, there's no one else it can be.'

'I can't believe you hadn't told them already,' Olivia scolded him. 'And what about the files? Had it all been backed up?'

'Yes, thank God.'

'Well that's something, one piece of good news.'

'There's more.' He shook his head, looking down at his plate. 'The contract with the council has been pulled. They reckon I haven't fulfilled my terms and have pulled the plug.'

'But surely you were doing things right, you are always so thorough?' Olivia was confused.

'I haven't got to the bottom of it but I suspect she has been busy in her new position there, making me look incompetent. Now I have an army of men to pay, at least until the next month, no jobs for them, and no money coming in. We could be ruined.' He looked up at Olivia and his eyes glazed over again.

'I'm sure you can sort it out. Get some sleep and look at it through fresh eyes tomorrow.'

Tom nodded sadly, too exhausted to think sensibly.

'And I've lost you.'

Olivia just looked at him but didn't reply. She saw the shell of the man she once loved, and whilst she still cared she couldn't help thinking he had brought it all on himself. How could she support him through this and be there for him when Sarah was at the bottom of it all, the one who he had made love to all those times while not thinking about her? In some ways it made her feel empowered to see that he was suffering. Why should she be the only one?

As she drove out of the gates later that evening she suspected that it was over. She let the tears flow but felt strangely calm. She never noticed the small red car that followed her all the way back to Claire's.

Chapter 60

The last thing that Olivia remembered was the headlights blinding her. She woke up in her hospital bed wondering where on earth she was, and why her friend was sat in the plastic armchair next to her, snoring.

'Claire?'

Her friend opened her eyes, glancing left and right before jumping up in her seat.

'Olivia, thank God you're awake, you had me worried.'

Olivia felt her head thumping and wondered if she was hungover, quickly deciding that she wasn't, that this was definitely a hospital bed, in a small hospital room, and no hangover was that bad.

'A hit and run, babe. Someone ran into you and left you out cold on the road outside mine.'

Olivia was speechless.

'Do you remember anything?'

She thought hard, the image of the headlights and

a flash of red paint, the sound of screeching, and then nothing.

'A red car, I think.' She looked down at her body to see if she had been hurt, but couldn't see any evidence of breakages despite the aches and pains. 'Have I broken anything?'

'No, hun, you had a full scan, just cuts and bruises. They were more worried about you being unconscious, but you came around briefly. I told them we'd just landed back from LA and you were probably just sleeping!' Claire laughed.

'Have you been asleep in that all night?' Olivia looked at the plastic chair that was definitely not made for comfort.

'Yep, see what a good friend I am, sleeping in a chair on landing day for you! Anyway I've phoned your mum, she's on her way up. I had better go and tell the nurses that you're awake.' Claire got up, looking a little stiff. 'Oh, and these guys want to speak to you.'

Olivia looked over to where Claire was pointing as two rather attractive uniformed policemen walked gingerly into the room.

Olivia couldn't tell them much, but they seemed interested in the bit about the red car, asking her if she was definitely sure about the colour. Olivia wondered who on earth they had in mind; she didn't know anyone who drove a red car herself. Maybe she had stepped out in front of it, she had parked as usual across the road from Claire's after all.

The day passed in a flurry of visitors. She sent her friend home to get a decent sleep, and her mum stayed until dark before heading off to stay at Claire's too. The nurses were pleased with her readings each time they came in to take them, but the doctor insisted that she stay in for one more night for monitoring. Just as she started to settle for the night, enjoying her first moment of peace that day, a knock on the door came, and it opened slowly.

First Sam and then Fiona walked in, looking like they had run her down themselves.

'Olivia I am so sorry,' said Fiona, still standing by the door, not coming any further into the room.

'Was it you, Fiona? Did you do this to me?' quipped Olivia, rolling her eyes theatrically.

Fiona looked at the floor and wrung her hands together. Sam put her arm around her sister's shoulders and gently pulled her into the room, closing the door behind them.

'Fiona needs to tell you something, Olivia.' Sam looked grave as she pulled a chair forward and sat Fiona on it. 'They've arrested Sarah, it was her who ran you down, and her who set fire to the office, it looks like.'

Olivia tried to take in what Sam was telling her. She wasn't surprised by the fire, but the fact that she had actually tried to run her over, tried to *kill* her, that was way too much to get her head around, and why was Fiona looking so worried?

'Fiona,' prompted Sam, sternly.

'I knew she was a bit nuts, but I had no idea how bad it was. I'm so sorry, Olivia, I should have told you what I knew when you asked.' She leant forward with her head bowed.

'Go on.' It was all Olivia could say.

'I knew she had had some trouble at home, that they wanted to send her here to get away from it, get a fresh start, but that was all I knew to begin with, honest.' She looked up at Olivia. 'But when you asked me if I could find out anything I'm afraid I lied to you. My friend did tell me she had caused big trouble at her dad's firm, something to do with his business partner. She had an affair with him, it seems, and was blackmailing him, then her dad found out and sent her here while things calmed down. The man's wife had wanted to call the police but Sarah's parents talked her out of it. It seems Sarah was always a little unbalanced, had been in counselling since she was a teenager, and her parents felt guilty about it, blaming themselves.'

'Why the hell didn't you tell me, Fiona?' Olivia wondered if she would have been able to stop any of it if she had known all of this then, or if it had already been too late.

'I'm so sorry.' Fiona looked at the floor again. 'My friend made me promise not to, and I had no idea she was causing any trouble, you just said you thought she was sad.'

Olivia nodded. She was right, perhaps if she had been honest herself and told Fiona exactly what her concerns were she would have opened up more.

'Her dad is booked on a flight to come over tomorrow, the poor family are in bits. I was supposed to look out for her and now they'll be visiting her in jail.' Fiona covered her face to hide her tears.

What a terrible mess it all was, thought Olivia. So many people's lives ruined, including her own.

Sleep was evasive that night; Olivia couldn't stop the images that flooded her thoughts. She could see Sarah's face, expressionless as she drove the car at her, and the image of herself being thrown to the floor repeated itself as if on a loop in her mind. Olivia felt scared again, laying in her bed with her lights on, even though she was sure Sarah was locked away.

Are you ok? It was past midnight when Tom texted. Olivia was relieved to have someone to communicate with.

No. She wasn't.

I'm coming over.

Despite everything that had happened Olivia couldn't tell him not to come, because right now she needed him there. She was scared, it made her feel small and vulnerable, and she needed Tom's strength right now. She thought for a moment that the nurses might not let him in as it was so late, but she knew that he would get to her.

What seemed like hours later, but was probably only forty minutes, the door opened and Tom appeared. He said nothing as he lay on the bed next to her and held her tightly. Olivia trembled as the anxiety and fear that she had tried to control came pouring out and he wept with her. They barely spoke, nothing needed to be said, but they found the comfort that they both needed right there in each other's arms.

As daylight crept through the curtains the sounds

of the rest of the ward waking up disturbed their slumber. A nurse came in to check on Olivia, followed shortly after by one of the policemen who had come the day before.

'We've arrested someone.'

'I know,' Olivia replied. He didn't need to tell her. He was interested to know how she had found out so quickly and she explained the connection, making sure that Sarah was locked away and not able to get to her again.

When the doctor came and told her that she could go home she didn't argue with Tom when he told her mum and Claire, who were back with her, that he would take her. She wasn't thinking of whether she was getting back with him, just that she needed him to protect her. Even her mum didn't say anything, just telling Olivia she could come to her when she wanted to. Olivia could see that Claire wanted to object but was grateful to her friend for not stepping in.

'I'll bring you over some of your things,' Claire said kindly.

'Thanks.' Olivia hugged her friend and then her mum before letting Tom lead her out to his car.

The next few days were surreal. Tom never left the house, Olivia staying in bed while her bruised body healed, and he watched over her quietly. Whilst he slept by her side at night, an invisible line lay between them, that only Olivia was allowed to cross in the times that she needed his strength. Her ring was still on the side where she left it, but she never put it back on.

Days and nights merged, until Olivia felt the haze lift and began to feel stronger. As the fear lessened she needed Tom less, and the resentment that his indiscretion had caused all of this began to build again. She saw the hope shatter in his face when she said she had to go, and could feel the pain in his eyes as he watched her leave once more. She felt lost as Claire drove her away, like she didn't belong anywhere, had lost her identity, and had her happy naive life stolen from her.

Chapter 61

Back at Claire's Olivia fought hard to get her life back to some sort of normality. It was hard to move on though, when she was constantly wondering about Sarah, and Tom. She was grateful more than ever that she was buddied up with Claire at work, as the anxiety was still with her and she worried how she would be on her own downroute.

'Rosters are out.' Claire jumped onto the sofa next to Olivia, clutching her phone. 'Let's see what holidays we are having in January.' She tapped in her passwords to get into the system. Olivia picked up her phone and started doing the same.

Olivia's roster timeline appeared on her screen.

'We got the Hong Kong!' squealed Claire. 'Brilliant, I hope the others got it.'

'Me too,' she said, seeing the HKG code. She scanned along – JFK, MCO, SEP. 'Ugh, I got SEP,' she complained. 'Please tell me they put you on that with me.'

'No, mine's not due till April, and as much as I

love you I'm not doing that four months early!' She laughed.

Olivia sighed; the last thing she needed right now was having to study those huge manuals and go through three days of exams and practicals. It was the biggest downside to the job, the annual recurrent, but if you didn't put the work in and pass there was a real danger of losing your job, and people did.

'Well I'm not studying until after Christmas.' It was early December and Olivia already felt sad about the upcoming holidays; she wasn't going to make it worse by doing that as well.

'At least we have New York, Orlando and Hong Kong though,' said Claire. looking over her shoulder.

'Do you fancy getting on a flight over Christmas with me? I don't think I can bear being at home.'

'Hell yeah, I was dreading spending it with my lot, all arguing!' Claire had five brothers and sisters and when they all got together it was quite rowdy. The girls had both been fortunate at first to have been rostered Christmas off when so many crew who wanted to be at home were having to fly. It would make someone's day when they offered to do their flight.

'How about Dubai? There are two crew here with it up for swap.' Claire was already looking on the swap page.

'Sounds great, a bit of sunshine, get us on it,' Olivia instructed her friend who set about getting things sorted.

'Done,' announced Claire ten minutes later, looking pleased with herself.

Olivia was distracted by the message that had just appeared on her phone from Sam.

Sarah's court date has been set for January 10th, thought you might like to know.

Although she had pleaded guilty, and Olivia didn't have to go, she knew that she needed to, that she needed to face her. Sarah's solicitor was putting in a plea of insanity or something akin to that, and Olivia worried that she may walk away free, despite assurances from her own solicitors that this wouldn't happen. January was going to be one hell of a month. Until it was over though Olivia felt stuck, like she couldn't move on, couldn't make any decisions while her head was so full. It really was a case of one day, one flight, at a time.

Chapter 62

'Are you sure you're up to this?' asked Claire. She was looking at Olivia seriously.

'Honestly, I'm fine, I can't take any more time off.'

Olivia closed her case and locked it. Despite the bruises that were now turning yellow beneath her uniform, she needed to get away. Being here was torturous, waiting to hear updates and going over and over things in her mind. There was also the money situation; she knew that she needed to start planning for her future, and even if she stayed with Claire for months she couldn't expect to live there for free. Whilst she would still get her basic salary if she went sick again, it wasn't very much, and like most crew she needed the extra money she got for each flight she operated. It hadn't mattered when she was with Tom, but now that she was supporting herself she needed every penny.

'Well let's go and get some sunshine then,' declared Claire, walking towards the door.

Olivia followed, pulling her case which felt light with its contents of summer clothes.

As they walked across the road to the car Olivia shivered, and wondered whether the wind had actually just picked up or whether it was her memory reminding her of that night. She opened the passenger door of Claire's car quickly, accepting her friend's help and letting her take her case to lift into the boot. The pain was bearable, and she wouldn't let it affect her work, but she was still grateful for the gesture. She wondered who the manager would be, and whether she would be able to mention her injuries, or whether she would have to keep a brave face on all flight lest she was berated for coming to work when she wasn't truly fit.

The display on the dashboard read eight degrees centigrade, and thick grey clouds blanketed the sky above them as they drove to the airport. She had been unable to lift herself from feeling as miserable as this day was for so long now, and hoped that the sunshine in St. Lucia would be enough to give her the break that she so needed.

'You'll all be getting an hour and a half crew rest,' Camilla paused and looked around at the mute crew, 'on the bus from the airport to the hotel.' She laughed, thinking that she had just made a joke, but no one else seemed to find the funny side. It was early, and the flight was nine hours long, so to hear that they weren't going to get any rest until they had landed just wasn't funny. It was lost on Camilla though, as she continued to deliver the briefing, completely unaware that the crew were not laughing and contributing as they did with other managers, only knowing what was normal for her flights and having nothing to compare them to, thinking that her way was the best way.

Camilla Thomas was possibly the most dreaded of all the managers, and Olivia had momentarily considered calling in sick at the last minute when she had seen her name on the crew list at check-in. It would have been so easy to run to the manager on duty and explain to them what had happened, cry a few of the tears that were so readily available lately, and get sent home, but she didn't. It was just a flight, she told herself, and she needed the two nights away. Anyway, after what she had been through lately she could handle Camilla. As she looked at the faces of the newer, younger girls and boys, she just hoped that they would be ok.

Olivia could see that Gemma was trying not to cry as she pulled her drinks cart back into the rear galley.

'Don't let her get to you, hun, she's just bitter and twisted,' Olivia said kindly, taking the cart from her and stowing it.

'She just shouted at me in front of the passengers.' Her voice wobbled.

Olivia shook her head.

'Honestly, I really don't know what her problem is, or how she's still here, she's been like this as long as I've known her. Please don't take it personally, she's always like it, hon, don't let her bring you down.' It was true, Camilla was notorious. She had been at the company for over twenty years and had forged herself a reputation as one mean lady. Apparently her peers remembered her as being quite sweet in the early days, but something had happened and she had grown bitter and twisted. It was her way to pick on the younger, more beautiful crew, and she wouldn't leave it until she had broken them. Olivia felt protective, almost maternal for this poor girl who hung her head and turned away, probably to hide the tears.

As Olivia prepared the carts for the meal service she wondered which of the many rumours were true about why Camilla had turned so mean. Was it the cheating ex, or the traumatic event...? She looked at the poor girl and felt angry; it didn't matter what had happened, there was no excuse. *Nothing* gave you the excuse to be horrible to people, to be mean, to hurt them. She rubbed the ribs that were still bruised and tried to calm herself.

'She's something else,' said Claire under her breath as she walked in the galley. 'She's just told a poor young lad off who got up to use the toilet. Poor thing was terrified, he didn't notice the seatbelt signs. His parents are fuming.'

Olivia shook her head, about to reply when Camilla walked into the galley. She was small and wizened, too thin, her face lined and aged with meanness, greying dark hair pulled back too tightly.

'Can we speed things up, girls? This service is taking a very long time.'

'What's the rush, Camilla? It's not like we are getting breaks so we may as well take our time and not hurry things.' Olivia wondered who had said it, and then realised it was herself; the thoughts that had been in her mind had just rolled off her tongue. She saw the look on Camilla's face, and rushed to find something to say first, to limit the damage. 'It's ok, Camilla.' She forced a smile. 'All of our passengers are very happy, we'll be out in just a minute. Gemma's just cleared in all of the rubbish and checked the toilets.' She could see Camilla trying to think of something to say back, but not finding anything to argue.

'Very well, I'm going back up to first class if you need me.'

'Oh, we're fine thank you, everything in hand down here,' Olivia called behind her as she left, still with the fake smile fixed to her face as she stuck up her middle finger, and carried on loading the meals from the ovens into boxes. Nothing more needed to be said, but the tension in the air was replaced with suppressed giggles as they all worked.

Chapter 63

The crew sat at the back of the coach carrying them from the airport to their hotel in Rodney Bay. It wouldn't have taken long to cover the distance on a motorway but as the aged vehicle crawled up the steep hills and drove slowly around the twists and turns of the narrow roads, the lush greenery and glimpses of the Caribbean Sea passed them slowly. Those on the crew who were familiar with this route had brought drinks for the journey, to make it go quicker, and they chatted merrily as they topped up their glasses. Even Camilla joined them, still oblivious to how they felt about her, thankfully seating herself next to the captain who was therefore forced to spend the journey talking to her. She seemed to lighten up though, Olivia observed, after a glass of bubbly. Perhaps the old her was still in there somewhere beneath the hard shell she had created for herself.

They howled with laughter at the game of charades that they were playing, and Olivia felt the warmth inside her, not from the sun that shone brightly in the sky, but from her love of these moments that she never took for granted. She looked around at the bunch of people who had mostly been strangers that morning, laughing like old friends on holiday. No one else outside of this job got to have these times and she felt truly blessed.

They drove slowly in the traffic through the town, marvelling at the cruise ships floating in the bay, looking so huge compared to the small buildings nestled in the hills behind them, and turned left into the road that led to their destination. They started to put their belongings away, gathering up the empty bottles and cans that lay around. As they drove into the hotel the view through the lobby out to the sea had never been so beautiful.

The thought hadn't crossed her mind until she stood in front of the bathroom mirror applying her sun cream the next morning. Her bikini failed completely to cover any of the bruises and she felt shaken and vulnerable again as she was reminded of what had happened. The mottled yellow and grey patches spread from her left shoulder all the way down to the bottom of her ribs, starting again on her hip and thigh. Apparently this was the side on which she had landed, the doctors had concluded, commenting that she had been lucky in some ways that the trauma to her head lay covered by her hair. Olivia was grateful for this, that her face had been spared, not because of vanity, but because she could cover the rest and to the outside world she didn't look like a victim. There were other, smaller bruises on the other side, probably from where the car had struck her.

She saw the sympathy in Claire's eyes as she stood in front of her.

'I can't go to the beach like this.' It had all been ok the day before, it had been dusk by the time they had arrived and she had quickly changed into her loose trousers and t-shirt. They had enjoyed happy hour at the bar and she had fallen into bed, not noticing the pain from the bruises anymore, so familiar with it now that it was almost normal. Now though, she was back in her reality again, and she resented that it was even managing to follow her here, tainting her enjoyment, not letting her forget. She saw her friend, ever the solution finder, think for a moment for a way to resolve it.

'I know. We'll find ourselves a couple of loungers at the end of the beach away from everyone. No one will notice that in your sundress, just take it off when you lay down.' Olivia knew this was the only option, there was no way she wanted to undress in front of the rest of them, knowing that they would all be shocked and feel awkward, not wanting to ask. She didn't want to talk about it, explain the whole awful situation to so many people.

'Oh my heavens, Olivia?'

Olivia had been enjoying the heat from the sun on her skin, listening to the waves and the rustling of the palm trees as the breeze blew their leaves. She had heard the light footsteps in the sand, and felt someone stand over her, but had resisted opening her eyes, hoping it was just a member of hotel staff and that they would just go away. Camilla's voice was like nails scratching a blackboard, making her wince before taking a deep breath and opening her eyes.

'What on earth happened to you?' Camilla looked shocked, but her tone was one that Olivia hadn't heard her use before, compassionate.

Claire had already sat up, and appeared ready to ask Camilla to leave, but Olivia looked at her with a smile that said it was ok and sat herself up slowly.

'It's not as bad as it looks, Camilla. I got hit by a car, that's all.'

'But darling you surely shouldn't be at work like that, you must still be in pain?'

Olivia gave in; she had been deluded to think she could avoid the subject for the whole of her trip, and she found herself telling this person who had been so frosty before, the whole sorry tale. Camilla just listened, never losing the look of sympathy, and nodding in understanding when Olivia justified why she had come to work.

'I wish you had said, we could have made sure you worked an easier position.' Olivia didn't like to tell her that her demeanour had not suggested a sympathetic ear.

Camilla looked like she might cry and to Olivia and Claire's astonishment proceeded to tell them about how she too had once been covered in bruises, at the hands of a man who had controlled her. She had been trapped for years in an abusive relationship from which she had finally found the courage to leave, but which she never felt truly free from. Olivia wondered if she often opened up, suspecting that she didn't.

Once again Olivia felt stronger when she got back from the flight to Claire's two days later. The sun had tanned her skin, and the bruises had almost gone. She felt almost like her old self, and she had a newfound resolve to take control of her life. Camilla had shown her what happens to those people who allow themselves to be eaten up by events, unable to put them in a box, in their memories, letting it twist them, but Olivia was good at storing memories away when she really needed to. She knew she would have to face the trial, and that she would need to face up to life without Tom in it, but she could start again, and she would.

Chapter 64

'You can just stay here, let's get all of this over with and then you can think more clearly about what you want to do,' said Claire.

A week had passed since they had got back from St. Lucia, and a quick flight to Boston had come and gone, just like Olivia's bruises. She still missed Tom terribly but there was no way that she could go back, despite his daily pleas, when all she could think about was Sarah and the upcoming trial. She felt like she needed to take back some control and so was trying to make her plan for the future, mindlessly scrolling through pictures of flats for rent. She had always known she was fortunate to live the lifestyle Tom had given her, and her heart sank as she looked at the small places that she could only just afford on her own. With no savings and a mediocre income it was unlikely she would ever be able to buy anywhere around here, and she wondered if it would be as unbearable as she thought to move back home where prices were much cheaper. Just weeks ago her future had been so certain and now she felt scared at having to start again.

'Thank you,' she said gratefully, she would much rather stay here with Claire than start again just now. Maybe when she had a clear mind she would be able to find a solution. The door buzzer rang and Claire walked away to answer it, returning moments later with a concerned look on her face.

'It's Tom, he's at the door.'

Olivia hadn't returned his calls or answered his messages for days, she had become numb to his words, but she felt panicked for a moment, wondering if she was strong enough to see him. She got up slowly, and walked tentatively to the front door where he stood with his head hung.

'Hi.' Tom sounded nervous as he looked up at her. 'I'm so sorry to just turn up but I needed to see you.'

'What do you want, Tom?' She didn't say it harshly, she couldn't be unkind to someone who looked so sorry.

'I don't know, I just needed to see you. I miss you so much.' He rubbed his face and looked up, blinking away the tears. 'Can I take you out somewhere? Will you come for a coffee, or dinner? Anything you want, but will you just come and be with me for a little while?'

'I can't, Tom.' Olivia could feel her voice faltering, and her lips trembled as she felt the emotion overwhelm her. The tears came and she didn't even wipe them away, and for a moment they stood and looked at each other in mutual despair. Olivia so wanted to fall into his arms, for him to hold her and make her feel better, but he was the one who had caused this so he couldn't fix it.

'I don't know what to do without you. Please tell me what I can do to make you come back?'

Olivia pictured their home, how happy she had been there, and then she pictured Sarah in it.

'I can never come back to the house, Tom, not after she was there.' Silence prevailed for a moment. 'It's over, Tom.'

Olivia wondered if she had actually just said those three words out loud, knowing that she had when she saw the glimmer of hope in his eyes go out. She moved to close the door.

'I'll sell the house, we can start afresh somewhere,' he said in desperation.

For a moment Olivia saw a solution to one of the hurdles, but it was just one of many, and not enough.

'I'll always love you, Tom, but I can't do this. I need to move on, I need to make a fresh start.'

Tom just nodded, standing steadfastly as Olivia closed the door. She wondered if he heard her sobs as she sank to the floor, and the gentle tones of her friend consoling her, picking her up and leading her away. She wondered if he felt the grief so deeply, suspecting that he did, that he was suffering as much as her.

It's over, Tom. She replayed the words in her head as she lay in bed that night, with tears still falling from her now swollen eyes. It was over, she had finally said it out loud, and she was grieving as if someone had died. She almost wished that he had died, at least then she wouldn't have the burden of hurt to carry on top of the feeling of loss. She had studied psychology at college and she tried to remember the stages of grief, hoping that she could get through them quickly, comforted to know it wasn't up to her to control it, that ultimately all humans would go through the same process, just at different speeds. Denial, anger, acceptance, or something like that, and she wished the days away until she could reach acceptance.

Chapter 65

Keeping busy had been the key to her sanity. The run-up to Christmas, with the visit home, the shopping and the flights had passed in a flash and as they landed in Dubai on Christmas Day Olivia felt almost herself. Tom had stopped calling and messaging and whilst it was definitely easier to move forward when he was out of sight and mind, she found herself checking her phone regularly and berating herself when she felt disappointed that there was nothing from him. She couldn't help wondering how he was today though, whether he would spend it alone, but she swept away the feeling of sadness, determined that she would not have a bad Christmas, despite everything.

For a country with a principal religion that did not recognise Christmas, they had still catered for those who did. The Christmas tree in the hotel lobby was magnificent, and the crew lined up in their uniforms for the Obligatory 'Christmas downroute' picture. Most of them were going to see family that were living out here, and the few of them who weren't made plans to meet for dinner that evening.

'Look at that view,' Olivia sighed as they walked into their room. The far wall was pure glass and the Dubai skyline spread across the horizon. The Burj Khalifa stood tall and proud, towering above the rest of the buildings. As she stood in the window Claire handed her a glass of champagne.

'Happy Christmas,' Olivia said, raising her glass, trying her best to feel in the spirit. She switched her phone on whilst Claire went for a shower and read the messages that popped up one after another with the same wishes. Her heart sank a little when she couldn't see one from Tom, but she knew that he was just doing what he thought was right, that he knew she needed to cut the ties completely in order to move on.

'Your turn.' Claire walked out of the bathroom in her white hotel robe, saving Olivia from her thoughts.

It was a little after four when the girls walked out of the hotel, and the warm sun welcomed them. They strolled along the promenade that swept around the man-made lake, with restaurants spilling out onto it from the mall behind. The crew were already sat around a table outside of the steak restaurant that they had chosen, all chatting merrily. It had been a busy flight over so Olivia couldn't even remember the first officer's name as she sat next to him, and she certainly hadn't noticed how good-looking he was until now.

'You look very nice,' he said approvingly, making Olivia feel a little shy. The dress she wore flattered her with its layer of navy chiffon skimming her curves, and its lace sleeves respectfully covering her shoulders so as not to offend the locals. She hadn't felt beautiful for a while now and his compliment was gratefully received.

'Thank you.'

'Sorry, I don't think we had a chance to chat on the flight, I'm Adam.'

'Olivia,' she replied, knowing that he had no idea of her name either. 'Sorry we were so busy, I didn't have a minute to get in and see you.'

The conversation was easy, but Olivia could feel that there was an undertone, that Adam was flirting with her. It wasn't the first time she had been flirted with by a pilot, but he was different, he seemed genuinely interested in her, and not like he was just trying it on with her for the night. He told her how he had just joined the airline after a working in the Middle East for a few years, and how he was starting a new life at home now after splitting with his girlfriend back in the summer.

The food and wine kept coming and before they knew it the sun had set. Olivia, who was sat with her back to the water, turned around as music began to play, and watched as the water fountains in the lake danced along with it. The light show was breathtaking, projecting its patterns and colours on the buildings around, laser beams cutting through the night sky. She could feel the warmth coming from Adam's body as he leaned close to her, and she didn't move away; she missed being close to someone.

'So, I have to ask. Do you have a boyfriend?' he asked as they sipped their coffees at the end of the evening. The rest of the crew were talking to each other and no one seemed to notice the familiarity that was growing between them. She noticed him looking down quickly at her hand, and presumed he was trying to see if she wore a ring.

'No.' Olivia felt a feeling, a pain, in her stomach as she said it. For the first time in years she really didn't have a boyfriend. Adam's smile didn't mirror whatever she was feeling, as she tried to work out what that was. Was it sadness, fear, or maybe just a sense of being lost?

'Oh, I can't believe you're single, it must be my lucky day.'

From most other men she may have found this a bit cheesy but something about Adam was different, it was ok hearing it from him. She felt her cheeks flush as she rolled her eyes derisively.

'I'm done.' Claire was standing over her, and the rest of the crew were getting ready to leave. Olivia stood up to join her friend, she was tired now.

'Are you not staying for one more drink with me?' Adam asked sweetly.

Olivia shook her head and smiled. It had been nice to feel wanted again, and maybe in a while she might be ready to date once more, but she wasn't yet. Adam looked disappointed, but was enough of a gentleman to not push it further.

'So, what was going on there?' Claire asked as soon as they were out of earshot. 'I think he likes you,' she teased.

'A bit soon, but yes, he's a really nice guy.'

'He certainly is. Not bad to look at either.'

Olivia just smiled. Although she doubted she would see him again she felt happy to know that there were still good guys out there, that Tom wasn't the last one. Maybe the future wasn't so bleak.

Chapter 66

January 10th had arrived so quickly. Olivia held on tightly to her mum's arm as they were led into the courtroom by the clerk and escorted to where they needed to sit at the back. The smell of wood from the panelling that seemed to line the entire room was overpowering and she felt lightheaded as she sat down. She had never been anywhere like this before but it was just like on the daytime TV shows, familiar even. She was grateful to Sarah for pleading guilty, that she wouldn't have to stand up and give evidence, be questioned even by the men in wigs who sat with their backs to her. In fact she didn't even have to be here, but she had come because she needed to hear her say it, admit what she had done, and see if she was sorry.

There were other people sat in the spectators' area already, and she mouthed hello to Fiona who sat a little way up from her. An older couple, maybe in their fifties, sat next to Fiona, looking straight ahead and holding hands. She thought she had seen them before somewhere but couldn't put her finger on where. The sad, worried looks on their faces told her that they knew Sarah, and she wondered if they were her parents.

Olivia stiffened, her pulse racing, as she watched Sarah being led into the room through a far door and into the dock. Sarah held her head up high, looking almost defiant, as the female officer with her steered her coldly into the seat. She was immaculately groomed as always, in a smart grey suit, as if she was just going to work, and Olivia felt a twinge of sadness when she saw that her hands were cuffed so crudely in front of her. The man who was sat with Fiona let out a loud sob and she saw Sarah look up. For just a moment she seemed to lose her composure, looking like a little girl as she looked back at him, until she saw Olivia, and the little girl was gone in an instant. Olivia saw the hate, the scorn that she held for her, and a cold shiver passed through her body as she realised that she wasn't sorry at all.

'All rise.' The call from the usher brought everyone back into the moment, and they stood as the judge appeared from a door on the opposite side to where Sarah had just come from. Dressed grandly in his gown and wig, he walked slowly to his seat in the centre of the platform and sat down below the Royal Coat of Arms that hung on the wall behind.

It was over in no time. She had watched Sarah as the charges had been read, trying to read her expressionless face, wondering what she was thinking as she sat there. She had pleaded guilty to both the arson attack on Tom's office and to the charge of Assault Occasioning Bodily Harm to Olivia, showing no emotion throughout. Olivia still couldn't believe that someone had wanted to hurt her that much, but whilst her mum had wanted her to be charged with attempted murder, she had been happy to believe that Sarah hadn't truly wanted that outcome that night. Now she wasn't so sure. A small part of her still couldn't help feeling guilty though. Perhaps if she had never got her the job, if she hadn't been so insecure herself, Sarah wouldn't have been pushed to it. Maybe it would never have happened and this beautiful but cold girl wouldn't be sat there now looking at having to spend her best years in jail. The sentencing was set for a later date and as she was led away they gathered themselves up silently to leave.

'Are you ok, Olivia?' Tom's voice came from behind her and she turned around to face him, wondering if he had been there the whole time.

'I will be,' she said back, hating the distance between them, that they hadn't been sat together, supporting each other like the other couple had.

'I'm glad it's over, that she can't hurt us – you – anymore. I'm so sorry.' Olivia looked at him. She saw the pain he was carrying, and realised he had been sentenced too for what he had done. 'Look after yourself,' he said sadly, nodding in recognition at her mum, who had stood silently behind her, and walking away. Again, the tears came and Olivia stood unable to move for a moment.

'Olivia.' Fiona's voice brought her back, and she quickly wiped her eyes before turning back around. 'Are you ok?'

'I will be,' Olivia said for the second time, convincing herself.

'Please don't feel like you have to, but Sarah's parents are here and they would really like to talk to you.'

Her gut reaction was to say no, absolutely not, until she looked over Fiona's shoulders and saw them there, looking so desperately sad. Now she remembered where she had seen them, in a photo, all those months ago, on Sarah's Facebook page.

Sarah's dad was a big man, strong, with grey hair thinning slightly on the top. Despite his size though, he looked small to Olivia, as if seeing his daughter like that had made him shrink. Her mum was beautiful, still slim and tall, an older version of Sarah; it should have been obvious when she had first seen them that they were her parents. She still held on to her husband for support as they sat at the table in the window of the bar ten minutes later.

'We are so sorry, Olivia, for what our daughter did to you. We never knew she was capable of going so far,' she said, shaking her head sadly.

Olivia nodded and felt her mum rub her back supportively.

'But we never should have sent her here, we should have let her face the music at home. Now she is in much worse trouble.' She let go of her husband and leant forward, clasping her hands together on the table and looking at Olivia. 'I'm so sorry to ask, but I need to know, what exactly happened, Olivia? Sarah won't tell us, and we need to understand.' She looked down sadly.

Olivia hesitated before taking a deep breath and

beginning to tell them. She felt herself stumbling over her words, telling the story that she hadn't expected to have to tell today, unprepared. She tried to explain to them in as few words as possible how Sarah had ended up hating her so much, how she had had an affair with her fiancé and had gone crazy when he wouldn't leave her. She left out the bits about how she had hated her too, and tried to get rid of her. Although she knew none of what she had done had justified Sarah's actions, she wondered if she would ever shake this guilt that she felt in her stomach, that she wasn't blameless.

Sarah's parents just listened, never questioning or trying to defend their daughter, as if they believed that she was capable of all of it, even without any provocation. When she had finished they all sat silently for a while, processing their own thoughts.

'Where is Tom now? Are you working through things?' asked Sarah's mum eventually.

'Oh, we split up.' Olivia was surprised at the question, surprised that they had asked it. Had they thought they could possibly have stayed together after everything she had just told them?

'Now listen my love, don't be too hasty. I know my daughter, and the bloke wouldn't have had a choice in the matter. Once she sets her eyes on something she always gets what she wants.' It was the first thing Sarah's dad had really said, and they all turned to him, waiting for him to go on. He shook his head slowly, gazing down at the untouched beer on the table that he was holding with both hands. 'I totally blame myself, letting her grow up with the lads at the yard, she had 'em right twisted around her little finger, and strewth, the trouble she caused when she got older.' He looked upwards, shaking his head.

'Go on,' said Olivia, needing to hear more.

'Love, there were too many times to tell you about.' He leant back, still hunching his shoulders. 'Every time she set her sights on one of the lads, it's like she didn't care who she hurt. Brian, geez, he tried to kill himself over her. He lost everything, left the wife and kids for her and she didn't even want him. But it's like she never learnt, never changed.' He looked defeated.

'She decided she was going to have Harry's partner,' Sarah's mum carried on for him. Olivia presumed Harry was Sarah's dad. 'And she got him. Stupid man couldn't say no. We were all best friends, he was always around our house having dinner with his wife, but Sarah never knew when not to cross the line. If she wanted something she had to have it.' Olivia was on the edge of her seat now, listening intently. 'He was a bit older though, and tried to get out of it, realised he'd made a mistake, but she wouldn't let him just walk away.'

'I knew something was wrong with him,' Harry continued, 'poor bloke, but I never thought he would have been such a galah.' He paused and took a sip of his drink. 'What I couldn't get my head around though, and still can't, is that my own daughter blackmailed him. She threatened to ruin him if he didn't leave his wife, and he believed it too.'

'So what happened?' Olivia was gripped, she needed to know the ending of the story. It was Sarah's mum who spoke first.

'What Sarah didn't reckon on was him telling his wife though, and her threats to break them up didn't matter then. She thought she knew everything, she'd never not got her way before. She was so angry.' She was looking out of the window now as she spoke, the emotion clear in her voice. 'She threatened all sorts, did some terrible things. They were going to go to the police, but Harry pleaded with them not to. That's why we sent her here, thought it was for the best.'

'So she came here and ruined *my* daughter's life.' Olivia could hear the anger in her mum's voice.

'It's ok, Mum.' She tapped the clenched fist that she had laid on the table. 'Did you not think she would do the same again?' she asked, looking at the pair of them despairingly.

'No.' Harry shook his head. 'I just thought it was with the lads at my work. We'd tried putting her into counselling and all sorts to make her see that what she was doing just wasn't normal. In the end I thought that perhaps the temptation at work was too much and that if she came here she'd get a nice normal job and a fella of her own perhaps. We'd hoped.' He looked at his wife who nodded in agreement, turning to look at Olivia. 'She was my little girl.'

Any anger Olivia had felt towards them for a brief moment was gone as she saw this strong man hurting. His wife rubbed his arm to comfort him and turned back to Olivia.

'We are so sorry, Olivia. Our daughter deserves what she gets now, but she is our child and we still love her. I think we will always blame ourselves for how she turned out.'

As they got up to leave they all shook hands cordially.

'What happened to your partner and his wife?' Olivia asked, realising she didn't know the true end to the story.

'They worked it out – she forgave him. They had too much to lose to let her take it away just because she could.' Harry held her gaze a little longer than necessary, making sure that she had heard what he said.

Chapter 67

Olivia had felt exhausted when they got back to Claire's, and by the time that she had told her friend about all that had happened she had fallen into bed and slept more soundly than she had for weeks. She tried not to think too much about the things Sarah's parents had said, her mind was too tired out after everything to think clearly. She would come back to it later but for now what she really needed was another break. As she packed the next morning for the trip to Hong Kong she felt relieved that it was now all over, and a few days away with the girls was exactly what she needed to start off the next chapter in her life.

'Girls.' Julie Margot's voice cut through the dull hum of noise in the terminal building. They had all met up a bit early to have a coffee before checking in, the four of them speaking quickly, all trying to catch up with each other and everything that had been happening in their lives. Olivia didn't want to dwell on hers; she had spoken enough about it recently, and listened happily to the others. They all turned to see Julie tottering over to them as glamorous as always, with a huge grin on her face. As she arrived at their table she went from one to another, kissing the air by their cheeks. 'Oh, I'm so happy to have such a lovey crew today, I can't tell you how much I have been looking forward to this flight. I do hope you've all brought something nice to wear on the night out.' She was obviously excited about what they would be doing.

'Of course,' said Ali. 'We can't wait, Julie. Shame we have to do the flight first, but hey-ho.'

'Fabulous.' Julie seemed pleased with the response. 'Well I'm going to go on down then. See you in the briefing, ladies.' And she was gone again, leaving a waft of her perfume suspended in the air around them.

The flight had been uneventful, as Hong Kongs usually were, and before they knew it they all sat in Julie's room with a glass of champagne in their hands and music playing over the portable speaker that sat on her desk. The captain, Nick, and one of the first officers, Graham, had come along for pre-drinks, along with a few of the other crew and the atmosphere was bubbling with excitement. Despite the long flight it was only early afternoon at home and everyone had plenty of energy for the night ahead.

'Have you seen this?' Nicola nudged Olivia and signalled in the direction of the window where the captain was sat. Julie was already monopolising his attention, not that he seemed to mind, but Lisa, the blonde lady who had been working at the front, seemed to want some of it too.

'They're having a blonde-off,' laughed Olivia, as she watched them compete. They were both of a certain age, both equally glamorous, and obviously not used to having competition on such a level playing field. The girls sniggered and turned away, leaving them to it. Olivia was intrigued as to how it would play out, suspecting that Julie would come out on top.

'Drink up then, everyone, we can't stay here all night.' It was Claire, taking the lead to get everyone moving.

Downstairs the bellman opened the doors to the taxis for them and directed the driver to take them to the mid-levels. A cocktail or two here would loosen them up nicely before heading down to Lan Kwai Fong. Olivia watched in amusement as the captain, with an inane grin on his face, was dragged by Julie into the last cab, away from Lisa, and she hoped that Lisa would do the best thing and step aside now before things turned ugly.

'Oh my god, can't someone tell her to give up?' Ali was coming back from the bar with a fresh round of cocktails. The girls were highly amused by the ridiculous look on the captain's face as the two blondes threw themselves at him. The threesome stood at the bar, almost glued to each other, and Olivia saw the fake smiles on Julie and Lisa's faces as they pretended to like each other, in denial of the competition that was obvious to everyone else.

'She's going to make her life hell on the flight

home if she doesn't back down soon,' said Nicola. The girls all nodded in agreement, knowing Nicola was right, that Julie would not take this lightly if defeated. Olivia suspected that it wouldn't happen though, that Julie, like Sarah, usually got what she wanted.

'He's bloody married as well,' Ali added. 'I had his wife on a flight once.' She shook her head. 'What's-a matter with some of these pilots? Can't keep it in their pants.'

'We're not all the same, you know.' They had forgotten Graham was sat on the table with them. 'But in his defence, they are throwing themselves at him!'

'Sorry Graham, I'm not suggesting you're all like it but it just annoys me when I see stuff like that.' She looked back at the bar.

'No offence taken, but it's hard for some to say no when it's thrown at them, that's all.'

Olivia felt herself being dragged down, her thoughts going to a darker place, relating this situation to her own. Even Tom hadn't been able to say no when it was thrown at him, but these guys were in this situation all of the time – Tom wasn't, maybe his was only a one off. His sad face came into her mind, how sorry he had been. That was what made him different to Nick, who wouldn't be caught, wouldn't be sorry, and would do it again. Nick still had a wife, he hadn't lost anything.

'Right, we're heading down the hill, see you in a bit,' Nick called as he passed with Julie on one arm and Lisa on the other.

'Catch you up,' Graham called back, tipping his glass to show he still had some to drink.

Another cocktail later and the rest of them linked arms as they struggled in their heels down the steep cobbled street. They were all very merry and Olivia bought the obligatory flashing headwear from the vendor, passing one to each of the girls. They stopped for photos outside of the bar where they were meeting the others before going in, and standing open-mouthed at the door as they saw Julie Margot swinging manically around the pole on the far end of the bar. The captain stood beneath appreciating the show, whilst Lisa looked poised ready to get up next and show what she could do.

'Oh, Christ on a bike,' said Ali, breaking their stunned silence.

Chapter 68

Jez laughed as Gabriella jumped up and down, cheering on her horse.

'Come on, Haymaker,' she squealed as the horses thundered past them heading for the finish line.

The stands at Happy Valley race course were full of people, some still in their suits after a day at work, others out for the night with friends, all cheering on their nags. The skyscrapers surrounding the venue reflected their lights downwards, and Jez wondered if people were stood in their apartments watching the events from behind the thousands of windows. Rock music played over the speakers and stalls with awnings that advertised the beers they were selling lined up along the edges of the track. He had never been here before, and this was probably the first time that he had come out with Gabby without feeling nostalgic and being distracted with thoughts of Ness.

'Yes!' Gabby threw her arms up triumphantly and turned around to see if Jez had seen her victory. He raised his plastic pint glass and tipped his head to signal that he had.

'I won!' she cried as she walked back towards him waving her betting slip.

'How much?' Jez asked cheerfully, knowing that it would be very little.

'Umm,' she said, studying her slip, 'fifteen dollars.' She looked up happily, before doing the sums and realising that fifteen Hong Kong dollars was in fact only one pound fifty.

'Drinks are on you then,' teased Jez, showing her his empty glass.

'Hmph,' Gabby protested jokingly, before heading towards their beer stall of choice. 'You can put the next bet on if you think you're so good, off you go,' she ordered, waving towards the top of the stairs where the betting took place. Jez did as he was told, chuckling to himself as he went. He and Gabriella had become close, she really did brighten his day.

'Jez, these are some of the guys I work with.' Gabby was stood with three men in suits when he came back from placing their bets. They shook hands and introduced themselves.

'We're going on to Lan Kwai Fong, you guys should join us,' said Bradley, the youngest of the three. Gabby looked at Jez, grinning and raising her eyebrows. He wasn't sure that it was really his scene, not that he had been there much, but he could see that she really wanted to go, and he wasn't ready to go home alone yet.

'Yeah, why not?' he said, pleased with himself when he saw how happy she was. 'I've got tomorrow off anyway.'

They waited for their last race, finished their drinks and followed the lads to the taxis that were waiting outside of the racecourse.

The pole dancing competition had ended abruptly when the captain had decided to take a turn, and been asked to leave by the angry Chinese bar lady. They had all left laughing, happy to go next door to Insomnia, another of their favourite haunts. The main part of the bar was open-air, spilling onto the bustling street. Doors at the back led into the where the band were playing, and a dancefloor, and more rock music blared each time someone went through them.

'I love this,' called Julie Margot, taking the captain's hand and dragging him into the dark club. Lisa followed them, still not giving up.

'Four lychee daiquiris please,' Olivia asked the barman, deciding for all of them what their next cocktail would be.

'Yummy,' said Nicola approvingly.

'Make that five,' called Graham.

'We need to go and have a dance after this one,' said Claire. Olivia could see that her friend was fighting the urge to play her air guitar, the inner rock fan in her trying to get out.

'C'mon then,' said Olivia, after handing the drinks out, which Graham had kindly paid for.

They walked through the doors and took a moment to adjust to the loudness of the music. Five Chinese boys with various instruments played the songs that everyone knew, the singer without a trace of an accent, a huge smile that showed he loved what he was doing as he sang to his fans. They spotted the others at the side of the dancefloor and Olivia was shocked to see that Julie Margot had taken her hair down and was frantically waving it around to the music. Lisa's short bob didn't have quite the same movement and she seemed to be giving up somewhat as the captain moved closer to the competition.

The girls laughed, always amused at how people behaved here, despite their everyday personas. In Hong Kong there were no inhibitions, no self-consciousness, everyone just let their hair down, literally.

The dancefloor was slippery with spilt drinks as they all jumped up and down and sang along, each of them feeling like the band was playing just for them. Olivia loved how happy everyone looked on the stage. Nowhere else, she suspected, would they get this level of appreciation.

'My round, be back in a mo',' called Nicola, taking everyone's empty glasses and walking off back through the doors to outside.

Chapter 69

Nicola came back ten minutes or so later carrying a tray with unknown cocktails balanced precariously on it.

'Look who I just found out there,' she shouted above the noise of the music, standing aside to let them see the pretty blonde that stood behind her.

'Gabby!' squealed Ali, rushing to give her a hug, followed by Claire. Olivia was confused, unsure why she didn't know her when all of her friends obviously did. She moved forward to take her drink from Nicola and looked at Claire.

'Oh blimey, sorry Olivia, I forget you weren't with us!' Claire apologised. 'This is Gabby, we met her here last time.' Gabby reached out her hand and shook Olivia's. Olivia warmed to her immediately.

'Lovely to meet you,' she said.

'This,' Claire paused as she used her thumb to point to Olivia, 'is our clumsy friend we told you about who should have been with us last time.'

'Oh, that friend,' Gabby nodded knowingly. 'It was

304

you who fell down the stairs.'

'Yep, that was me.' Olivia raised her hand in ownership as she sipped her drink through a straw.

Someone tall walked up behind their new friend, but Olivia was looking down at her drink so she didn't recognise him until she heard his voice.

'There you are, I wondered where you'd gone.'

'Sorry,' Gabby apologised. 'These are the girls I told you about ages ago, that I met down here, the flight attendants that I had such a good night with.'

Olivia froze with her straw in her mouth; she wanted to look up but couldn't, her stomach was flipping over and she couldn't compose her thoughts.

'Jez, this is Claire, Ali, Nicola and Olivia.'

Olivia looked up slowly, knowing what she was going to see, Jez looking back at her with the same level of shock that she had felt. It hadn't occurred to her, crossed her mind even, that she would bump into him. All thoughts of him had been buried underneath all of the other stuff that had happened recently.

'Olivia, I can't believe it's you.' Jez broke the silence. 'How are you?'

'You know each other?' Gabby looked confused, as did Olivia's friends who were all stood watching the pair of them struggling with how to act with each other. Olivia had never told even her closest friends about Jez; she had been ashamed of herself for how she had felt and what she had done.

'Yes, we met once before. Olivia was working on a flight I came back on with Mum and the kids, then she joined us for Tilly's tea party in the park.' Olivia was grateful to him for explaining it all so innocently.

'You never mentioned any tea party in the park.' Claire was looking at her intently. She knew that her friend knew that there was more to the story, that she would have told her about it otherwise.

'I love this song,' said Gabby, handing Jez her glass to hold. He barely took his eyes off of Olivia as he took it from her. Nicola had put her tray down by now and followed the rest of them into the throng of people dancing, all except Claire hadn't noticed or suspected that there was anything more than an acquaintance between them.

'How are you?' Jez asked now that they were alone.

'Good, thanks.' Olivia felt sober, back down to earth, and still with this feeling in her stomach.

'Shall we go outside to talk? It's a bit loud in here,' Jez suggested. Olivia nodded in agreement, feeling nervous as she followed him out.

It wasn't the night that Olivia had expected to be having but as she relaxed she began to enjoy Jez's company again. She remembered why she had liked him before, only this time she was single, and she wasn't sure how she should act and feel now that it was ok to be here with him.

The others came in and out for more drinks, disappearing quickly each time back to the dance floor.

'Oh, mate, you've gotta come and see what's going on in there,' Claire said, interrupting their conversation. Olivia and Jez both rose and followed her through the doors.

It took a while to focus, to see what Claire had been talking about, until she saw the group of them in the middle. Julie Margot's dancing had slowed down, and she was now dancing alongside Lisa, in alliance. The captain, meanwhile, had had all of his attention diverted to the pretty blonde who had joined them. Gabby was oblivious, lost in the music and the atmosphere, not noticing Nick gyrating around her. Olivia laughed, momentarily embarrassed for him, thinking he looked like a tropical bird trying to attract a mate with his complex dance routine.

'I'm so sorry for my colleague's behaviour,' she laughed to Jez. He was laughing too, but not right up to his eyes, and Olivia guessed that not everybody understood this kind of situation.

If she had been writing the story Olivia would have presumed that she and Jez would start where they had left off, but despite enjoying his company again something stopped her taking it forward. Neither did he push for anything more; the connection that they had both had before didn't seem to be there this time. The drinks flowed and the conversation was easy, but when he said goodbye it was like they were old friends.

'I had better get Gabby home, I think she's had enough,' he said as Gabby came out with Claire, hanging on to her and rolling her head.

'It was lovely to see you again.' Olivia hugged him, feeling his warmth and liking it, enjoying the embrace for that brief moment.

'You too.' He looked down at her, right into her eyes. Nothing more needed to be said.

'Bye,' called the girls in unison, waving the pair of them off.

'My round,' Olivia said assertively, needing to get back to that carefree stage she was at before they had arrived.

'So, who is Jez?' Claire asked accusingly.

'I'll tell you another time,' said Olivia. Jez was no one, just an acquaintance.

Jez put his arm around Gabby in the back seat of the cab, letting her lean against him, and kissed the top of her head gently. It was funny, he thought, he had held Olivia on a pedestal as the only one who could get him over Ness, but she wasn't the only one after all. When he had seen that drunk pilot all over Gabby on the dancefloor he had felt protective, uneasy, jealous even. He hadn't noticed how his feelings for her had been growing, he didn't recognise them as they were so alien to him now, but here she was in his arms and it felt so right. Olivia had been the one to open him up to the possibility of moving on, but Gabby was the one he wanted to move on with. He smiled as he saw the light at the end of his long dark tunnel.

Chapter 70

The trip had been a blast. They had stayed out till sunrise, watching the tai chi in Victoria Park before going to bed. They laughed through their hangovers the next evening as they wandered around the shops in Causeway Bay, and when the wake-up call rang on their phones the next afternoon Olivia felt lighter than she had in ages, ready to go home.

The flight was long, and Olivia was on first break. She had slept so well in the hotel that she wasn't tired, and she lay in her bunk with her eyes open, staring blankly at the light controls on the sidewall. For the first time in weeks she allowed the thoughts to come without pushing them away; she felt ready to deal with them, and as they came one after another she saw them clearly. She saw Tom, broken, sorry and so sad. She compared him to the captain and saw that they were so different. She saw Jez, how she too had made a mistake once, albeit smaller, but how she had resisted it this time, even though she was apart from Tom now. She played over the words of Sarah's parents, and as she finally drifted off to sleep she went in her mind back to her home, her happy place and her happy life.

'I'm just popping out.' Olivia pulled up outside of Claire's and opened the boot, only taking out her friend's suitcase. Claire looked at her confused.

'Where?'

'Tell you later.' Olivia didn't have time to explain, or justify, but she needed to be somewhere really quickly.

Claire stood on the pavement looking bewildered as Olivia closed the boot and drove off.

Olivia drove across town in a state of urgency. She didn't think she had ever felt so desperate. Every red light was an enemy and she weaved in and out of traffic like a racing car driver.

The buzzer rang and for a moment her heart sank when no one picked up. She pressed it again.

'Hello?' came his voice.

'It's me.'

The gates opened and Olivia drove in, abandoning her car in front of the house as the door opened.

'I want to come home,' she said quietly, hoping that he still wanted her there.

Tom stood in the doorway with a look of disbelief on his face, before it crumbled and he stepped towards her, picking her up in his strong arms and holding her so tight she could barely breathe. She felt his tears on her neck, and cried her own onto him. She knew he had suffered enough, that he would never do anything like that again, and neither would she. When he carried her through the door she felt elated. As Sarah's dad had said, Sarah took things because she could. Well this was *her* life, and she was taking it back. Because *she* could.

THE END

Printed in Great Britain
by Amazon